FERTS

GRACE HUDSON

This edition published in 2016
Copyright © Grace Hudson
All rights reserved.

The moral right of the author has been asserted.

ISBN-13: 978-1530816675
ISBN-10: 153081667X

Printed and bound by Createspace
DBA of On-Demand Publishing, LLC
www.createspace.com

Cover Design by Sanura Jayashan
Interior Formatting by GH Books

Sign up to the Grace Hudson newsletter:
www.gracehudson.net
Twitter: @gracehudsonau
Facebook: www.facebook.com/gracehudsonauthor
Goodreads: www.goodreads.com/gracehudson

This edition is also available in e-book
978-1-943279-52-4

This book is dedicated to my partner.
For listening,
encouraging,
watching
and waiting.

1

"Sound it."

"Sir?"

"I said sound it. Another has escaped."

The siren hummed through the surrounding forests, a rumbling whine that grew in volume as the minutes passed. Many could say they knew how to resist the pull of the Ward Beacon, but they were in the minority. An Internee had once attempted to remove her own eardrums in a vicious effort to get free of the perimeter zone. She was recaptured within hours, patched up and left to recover in Zeta Circuit. Zeta housed the defective, the damaged, it was the station for the used. Once admitted to Zeta, there was no means of promotion, no advancement opportunities. Zeta was the end of the heap, the end of hope.

Officer Cerberus glanced outside the immediate perimeter. The dryness of the day had given way to mist, the change permeating the air with a promise of a smattering of rain.

"Only one?"

"Sir?"

"Is that all you can say?" Cerberus huffed, turning his head in annoyance. The young operator, Quinton, looked up at him with wide eyes.

"I'll start again. Is. There. Only. One."

"Escapee? Yes, Officer. Only one. Internee Beth 259251, 19Y, Epsilon Circuit."

"Then she's not a high priority. Nonetheless, get her back. We have the highest recapture rate for this quarter. Keep it that way."

"Yes, Officer."

Cerberus strode out through the rear of the observation tower, leaving Quinton to his track and surveillance duties. The console zoomed in through trees to show the clear, glowing bright red outline of a young Internee, bent at the waist, visibly panting. Her hand gripped the tree beside her as she crouched, other hand planted firmly on her right knee to steady herself. She had lasted all of two minutes, the Ward Beacon surely must be having some kind of effect on her implant marker by now. Quinton looked more closely through the cracked monitor, admiring the sharp outline of her jaw, the defiant spread of her shoulders, as she leaned back against the tree, resisting the call.

"Go back," he whispered.

She raised her head, as if sensing something.

He checked her file in the logs, Epsilon Circuit, three years trained, two years fight duty. Beth 259251. They were all marked as Beth, only the numbers would change between Internees. She was assigned to Epsilon Circuit due to a hormonal imbalance at fourteen. She had contracted a common autoimmune disorder, causing her fertility rating to drop to a 5.6, but it was her muscle mass that relegated her to the betting Circuit of Epsilon. Her muscle mass was far above regulation and despite her condition she was physically strong, testing high on agility. Her fight record was exemplary, a formidable opponent for any challenger from the Epsilon Internee fight pool.

The endurance monitor blipped. Her heart had begun to stutter. She had five, maybe six minutes to get back within the ward zone before her time ran down.

"Back, come on," he muttered. It was none of his concern, certainly nothing he would voice in front of the other Operators for fear of derision. The Internees were plentiful, and the common Epsilon fellows were worth far less than the price of a basic ration.

The endurance monitor spiked, displaying elevated cortisol and increased respiration. She clung to the bark under her fingers, scrabbling for equilibrium. He had seen this routine so many times before and had grown tired of the spectacle. He could do without another demonstration tonight.

Before long, Beth 259251 stood to her full height, appearing to move towards the ward zone. Quinton exhaled, shifting back in his seat, ready to log her return. She hesitated, then turned to face the sparse plains of the suspension zone. Each small step was heavy, but she persevered, dragging her body further from the tower reach. The beacon's steady hum permeated the forest. Her hands crept up to cover her ears, routinely dropping back down in futility. One minute and forty-five seconds later she dropped to her knees, heart rate spiking, shuddering. The endurance monitor blipped once last time as her form faded to a dull green on the console.

"Recovery detail, suspension zone border." He called out the coordinates into his radio, ignoring the crackle, repeating the details to ensure they had been received.

"Confirmed, Quinton. Log response time at 18:16."

"Proceed as logged," Quinton replied. He hissed a breath out through his teeth. The Epsilon fellow was no longer his concern.

2

The FERTS facility was utilitarian in nature. To the outside, FERTS was indeed the high-tech, glossy boutique promoted in the presentations used to lure in prospective Vendees. The FERTS facility lay in the heart of the suspension zone perimeter, certified forbidden territory for all Resident Citizens. The image projected by FERTS was miles of white, marbled, downlighted department-store chic, with attractive Internees from Beta Circuit dressed in white jumpsuits, smiling into each new camera with renewed pep and enthusiasm.

The Vendees could be mistaken in thinking that the entire complex was set out in a similar fashion, gleaming white, polished chrome, scrupulously hygienic and fashionably sterile. The Vendees could also be mistaken in believing that all the Internees were just like the visible examples. Bright, healthy specimens with large white smiles, twinkling eyes and a dutiful nature. What the Vendees could not possibly deduce was that the Internees were carefully selected Show Internees, the most dutiful, the most attractive, and most importantly, the best at projecting a sense of contentment, joy and genuine happiness. The real FERTS, however, was something entirely different.

The FERTS Internees who were ultimately chosen as Vassals were paraded to each township for Vendee purchase, where The Resident Citizens enthusiastically engaged in the process of outbidding each other, trading furs, grains and fruits, crude weaponry and cider. Once sold, a Vassal became the sole property of the Resident Citizen for a designated period of time. A Vassal was returned to FERTS once the Resident Citizen grew tired of the Vassal, or the Vassal reached the over-limit age of 26Y. A Vassal was also returned in the event that a Vassal became a birther. A Resident Citizen needed no part in the process of birthing, and would only require Sires, who would then grow up to become Resident Citizens. If the result of the birthing was female, the prospective Vassal would become an Internee, assigned to Beta, Omega, Kappa, Epsilon or Zeta, dependant on general health, potential attractiveness rating and probable fertility prospects.

The complex was coordinated based on two criteria. Firstly, and most importantly, was the criteria of physical attractiveness. All Internees with a physical attractiveness score of more than 8.2 were placed in Beta Circuit, regardless of all other ratings. The most attractive were picked most frequently by the Vendees and fetched the largest amounts at sale, whereas other factors were less often discussed. An Internee's attractiveness was based on simple criteria, height, weight, muscle mass, configuration of features and overall appearance of health. Those deemed to be most attractive were over regulation height of five feet six inches, a minimum of muscle mass, an overall slender and streamlined appearance, with wide-set eyes, a straight thin nose, and wide, well proportioned lips. Teeth were to be straight and white, with good mineralization and strength. Eyes were to be clear, eyelashes long, and hair thick and glossy. The Internees were taught to keep their muscle percentage to a minimum, so as to maximize their attractiveness rating. The Officers and Operators, however, knew that the Internees who were thin and less well-muscled were by far the easiest to restrain and contain. Any Internee who was found to have developed a skeletal muscle mass of greater than 24.3 were sent on compulsory transfer to Epsilon Circuit to participate in the games. Once relegated from Beta, an Internee could never return to that coveted position. The highest a relegated Internee could climb would be to Omega Circuit, the second tier of the Apex in the FERTS hierarchy.

FERTS stood for Fertility Emigration Resource and Training Supply, the sole source of female Vassals for the town's male Resident Citizens. Vassals were plentiful, and were routinely sent out to prospective Vendees in a horse-drawn cart, secured with a wooden cage. Vassals were sold from the age of sixteen and up to the age of twenty-six. There were no Vassals marked for sale over the age of twenty-six.

The second criteria, and considered second in importance, was that of fertility. Each Internee was periodically tested for hormonal balance and fertility probability based on age, hormone levels and reproductive organ health. The score would determine viability for birthing, once the attractiveness ratings had placed each Internee in the appropriate Circuit. Scores of 8.5 and above determined the overall viability of an Internee's suitability for sale to Vendees.

Those with a fertility score of 9.6 and above, with a physical attractiveness score of 8.2 or more were assigned to Beta Circuit, which housed the most aesthetically pleasing of prospective Vassals to be and all active birthers sent from Vendees. All Vendees sent their Vassal back to FERTS should a birthing cycle occur and opted to choose a new Vassal rather than reclaim the original after the cycle was completed. Actions such as these were encouraged by FERTS Relations Officials, since most Vendees had no interest in the Vassal's body after the birthing cycle and tended to return them anyway. It was only logical to find a younger Vassal as a replacement and save on the needless administrative costs.

The 7.9s and above resided in Omega Circuit, a respectable gathering of prospective Vassals and the second choice for most of the less affluent Vendees. These Internees were constantly encouraged to relentlessly work on their appearance, through restricted nutrition, exercise and continual grooming practices. If an Omega was to put in the required effort, and should their attractiveness rating be amended, then an Omega could make the transfer to Beta.

All those who were not deemed to be sufficiently aesthetically pleasing were relegated to Kappa or Epsilon, depending on their physical strength and capabilities.

Internees from Beta and Omega who increased their muscle mass above regulation levels were automatically relegated to Epsilon, regardless of previous attractiveness ratings. Epsilon was the Circuit of chance, and all Internees relegated to Epsilon had failed to reach the standards of physical attractiveness or fertility required to become a Vassal ready for sale. Epsilon Internees had special abilities based on speed, agility, strength and cunning.

Epsilon Internees were scheduled to fight, often to the death, for the purposes of betting and entertainment. The Officers were the most frequent attendees, however, many wealthy Resident Citizens paid for the privilege of hosting their own personal games, often purchasing one or two of the winning Internees for fight scheduling within the confines of a private domicile. Many lavish parties were held, where Resident Citizens were entertained by Epsilon Internees, taken for pleasure and then used for sport, fighting until one emerged victorious. Epsilon Internees were not expected to return, and all were marked as expired as soon as the terms of sale were negotiated.

Down from Epsilon came the 6.5s and below, who were assigned to Kappa, consisting of those unlikely to be chosen as a Vassal. These Internees made up the labor Circuit. The work was physically demanding, dirty, and without any discernible reward. Many who could no longer fulfil their duties in Kappa were sent to Zeta Circuit, the bottom rung of the Circuit hierarchy.

Zeta Circuit was rarely mentioned. Most of the prospective Vassals knew nothing of Zeta Circuit, the idea merely a distant reminder of how lucky they were to be in their respective Circuits. Beta and Omega Circuit were kept uninvolved in any news or knowledge of Zeta, all that most of the Internees knew was that Zeta was the lowest Circuit, the one from which none would graduate. A ticket to Zeta Circuit was one-way, and no Internee, regardless of station, cared to dwell on the concept for too long. Zeta housed the sick, the lame, and those no longer able to work in the Kappa rotation. The Zeta Internees were kept separate from all other Circuits, and it was widely whispered that Zeta was the only transfer option for those who had reached the over-limit age of twenty-six. Nobody knew for sure, as Zeta was the only non-aspirational Circuit, meaning that those who were relegated to Zeta would never raise above the Circuit to reveal other Internees of the conditions there. For many, Zeta remained a mystery, and many were determined to know as little about the Circuit as possible. The Officers, Operators, Prospective Vassals and Internees knew well that this was a fundamental fact: Zeta was for the losers, and all within deserved the scorn and derision afforded to them.

3

Beth 259201 turned her head, blearily glancing around her chamber. The walls were regulation white, with a large bed, bedside table, bathroom, table and chair. Music filtered into her consciousness, bland and inoffensive, designed to soothe and relax. Most of the time it just annoyed her. There was a thin window, too thin for her to fit through, just enough to allow the air to flow and on certain days, it wafted through the foreign scents of the forest below.

She stirred, snuffling into her regulation silk slip pillow. All Internees were supplied with silk to minimize creasing for presentation. She saw no sense in it, considering she had been relegated to Epsilon twelve months ago for breaking muscle mass regulations. Her muscle mass last month had tested at 30.1, far too high for any kind of promotion. Beth 259201 had been a Beta Internee, rated attractiveness 8.9. Her features were pleasing, according to the adjudicating Officers, and her general health was rated as excellent. Her intelligence was far above the required limits of testing. However, she had excelled in none of the required activities except for training drills and general exercise, and her penchant for spending too much time in the regulation gym had resulted in her demotion to Epsilon. Her regulation red Epsilon jumpsuit hung over a chair, however the insignia bearing her identification had changed. Yesterday it had read 259201 23Y. This day it read 259201 24Y.

She sat upright, facing her evaluation mirror. Her long dark brown hair hung in a shaggy mop, never smoothing and curling around her shoulders like her grooming Officers had specified as a requirement. Her slanted hazel eyes blinked back at her, slightly puffy from lack of sleep. Her light olive skin appeared dulled today. Her morning Epsilon beauty pill lay waiting in her small bedside tray. She hastily took the pill, following a long drink of water. She made a mental note to remember to increase her fluid intake this week. She knew how it looked, her sullen features glowering back at her. Her attractiveness rating would be readjusted at this rate. She had rated poorly on grooming, dutiful activities and sexual availability. In fact, she had not even attempted the eyelash fluttering, simpering, smiling or any of the other signs of availability taught to her fellow Betas. She could not convince any of the Officers that she was interested in them, nor could she convince herself. So she declined to try, much to the chagrin of her instructing Officer, Harold.

Later that morning, he had taken her aside in one of the small assessment rooms and made her predicament clear.

"201. If you continue like this you know what will happen. You will stay in Epsilon and before long you will qualify to be a Fighter. Once you are scarred, you cannot return to Omega."

"I know. Yes. I understand. I just can't pretend like that. I don't mean it. I don't like... I mean, I'm not interested. At all." 201 cast her eyes downwards, studying her regulation Epsilon boots.

"Whether you are interested or not is irrelevant and you know it. You must try harder."

Harold was a patient Officer. His grey beard and quiet demeanor made 201 feel safe somehow. His insignia glowed back at her, 62Y. He had never tried to make any advance towards her in a sexual manner, but 201 knew from experience that this was no guarantee of what may happen in the future.

"You're a 24Y, 201. You don't have much time left. You have tested higher in intelligence than most other Internees I have seen in my time. But this is not what you need, these skills will not help you here. You need to excel in all required areas so you can be presented as a Vassal. I don't think you understand how important this is to your development." He took a moment to scribble indecipherable notes on his clipboard. He sighed, leaning forward in his chair, evaluating her appearance.

"You don't even brush your hair. Look, you even have a tangle here. It's disgraceful." He pulled on the matted strands to hold them in front of her face, expression stern.

"It's a waste of time," 201 muttered.

He stared at her, unimpressed. "And your nails, they are just too short. And unpainted."

"They get in the way of..."

"Do you even use the regulation skin cream? You look a little dry around the eyes."

"No I don't, well, sometimes. No, not really."

"It's not good enough. You know that 201."

"But... "

"No buts. And work on your attraction technique. It's terrible."

"Yes, Harold." 201 struggled not to roll her eyes. Harold was a kind man from what she had seen, but she had no desire to test that theory.

"I should like to see you out of here, out of Epsilon. Do you think you can try, for me?"

"Why?"

"You ask too many questions, I told you that before. Can you do this, for me?"

201 thought for a moment, weighing up her non-existent options.

"Okay, but only for you, Harold." She smiled sweetly, batting her eyelashes.

"And no sarcasm. You may think you are able to fool them, but not me." 201's face fell. She really was terrible at this.

4

Cerberus hesitated, pausing outside the finely carved door. The rooms were always dark at this time of the evening. The Pinnacle Officer's rooms were tucked away in the highest level of FERTS, access by special arrangement only. Few Officers, let alone Operators, were granted access. His personal domicile covered much of the top floor of the complex, plushly decorated in shades of magenta and mahogany. The entrance to the main study was flanked by two Officers, dressed in black, faces stoic. Their large frames dominated the atrium housing the entrance to Wilcox's main office. Neither of the Officers made eye contact, but he knew they observed every minute detail of his movements as he readied himself for the regular review update. He checked his clipboard one more time, then knocked.

"Come."

"Sir." Cerberus entered the study, eyes adjusting to the darkness within. Pinnacle Officer Wilcox sat in his usual corner, smartly dressed in casual Officer issue. His clothes were silver, unlike the rest of the Officers, and his shaved head caught the glow from his desk lamp as he looked up at the Officer before him.

"Cerberus. Please. Take a seat." He gestured to a smaller seat at the end of the desk. Cerberus promptly sat, sliding the clipboard across the desk for perusal.

"Three escape attempts this month. All recovered." Wilcox nodded subtly, turning to the next page. If he had noticed that Cerberus had failed to use the term 'recaptured', he made no indication.

"That all?"

"Sir. The list of Zeta recommendations." Wilcox flipped to the next page, scanning the long list of names, his eyes rested on the figure at the end of the page.

"Hmm." He smoothed his hand over his ear, rubbing his thumb idly over his mouth. "Up to thirty-seven this month. That is acceptable. Birthers?"

Cerberus reached out for the clipboard, then thought better of it, retracting his hand. "Fifteen. Three expired."

"Sires?"

"Five."

"Lodge the transfer orders for Resident Citizen placement for the Sires."

"It has been done. The Vendees and school placement heads have been informed."

"Any potentials from the rest of the new pool?"

"Two with good potential birthing prospects, birthers were Beta, 8.2 Vassals and above."

"Keep these two only. Transfer the rest to Zeta. Is that all?"

"Yes. Thank you, Sir." Cerberus backed out of the room, eyes steady as Wilcox returned to The Beth

Register on his undamaged but dusty screen, scrolling through the marked shortlist. The Beth Register listed all Internees in Beta, Omega and Epsilon, detailing their attractiveness ratings and compiling a listing of each Internee's characteristics.

"Oh, and Cerberus?" He clicked on a key, as the screen displayed a Beta Internee, a blonde with blue eyes. Her statistics loaded crudely one by one around her image, numbers appearing in each box, illuminating the screen with a green glow.

"Let's see." He clicked again, zooming in on her shapely legs. "Send up Beth 259212."

5

201 retired to her chamber after night rations. She sat on her bed, seduction technique manual laid out before her. The first page was simple, at least for her former fellow Internees at Beta. It seemed she was always trying to catch up, while the others just seemed more... natural at seduction.

The first page read: 'When interacting with a potential Vendee, a Vassal must lower the head, always looking upwards in deference, half closing the eyes to accentuate the lashes. A Vassal must speak only when asked to do so.'

201 rolled her eyes. She could not seem to grasp the concept of waiting for permission to speak. Sometimes she had so much to say, it seemed nonsensical to seek approval for the privilege. Harold was certainly vocal in his disapproval of 201's predilection for speaking out of turn, and he was unimpressed with her lack of skills when it came to her professed enticement and charm. No matter how 201 looked at it, she could not ascertain how she would overcome this obstacle to promotion back to Omega and her possible conferral of Vassal status. Becoming a Vassal was the ultimate distinction for

any Internee, though only Betas and Omegas were given this chance. At present, 201 was saddled with her status at Epsilon, her promotion to Fighter looking like the only possibility for advancement at this stage in her development. Once she received nomination for the Epsilon Chance Wheel, she could, potentially, become a Fighter and receive the acclaim of FERTS through victories in the Epsilon Games Ring.

201 reluctantly turned to the next page, steeling herself for the insights within. 'A Vassal must be understanding of her status at all times. A Vassal must show submission to all potential Vendees, Resident Citizens, Officers, Operators and Sires.'

201 blew out a breath, disheartened. She muttered sardonically to herself, the words sounding through her empty chambers. "A Vassal must show submission to... basically everyone. Except other Vassals. A Vassal may show authority over non-Vassals, and Internees of Epsilon, Kappa and Zeta Circuit. Though nobody has ever seen a Zeta Circuit Internee, unless they are, themselves relegated to Zeta Circuit, and therefore, there is not much need to feel superior to anybody."

201 turned the page, pressing on, despondency setting in.

You should know this by now. You have been learning this since you were a little one. Why can't you assimilate this information like all the others before you?

'A Vassal's sole purpose is to provide pleasure to their Vendee. If it is the will of the Vendee, then it is the Vassal's duty to provide birthing duties. The results of this birthing are the sole property of FERTS, and FERTS holds the authority to make any decision deemed necessary in such matters.'

201 scrunched up her nose at the prospect. She had seen birthers in Beta, their faces radiant with barely contained pride, holding the little ones tightly and petting their tiny heads, the other Beta Vassals crowding and exalting their achievements. The little ones did not stay with the birthers for long, 201 noted. The Sires were treated with the utmost reverence, the others were paid little regard. The birthers did not seem to mind when the little ones were taken, pleased with their duty to FERTS as a Vassal and a birther. They had reached the height of distinction, and could be duly proud of their achievements.

201 knew that she did not wish to be a birther, though Harold and many others had made it clear that her wishes had no bearing on the matter. Perhaps Harold was right, 201 just needed to learn the information that she had conveniently ignored as much as was possible up to this point.

"Concentrate, 201."

She turned the page, struggling to empty her mind and simply absorb the information on the page in front of her.

'If a Vassal is given a request from a Vendee, a Vassal must comply unconditionally. A Vassal must treat each word from a Vendee as a command, and a

Vendee will not enjoy making a request twice. A Vassal must comply with each and every need of the Vendee, without question.'

201 skipped a few pages, growing tired of the endless requirements.

'When a Vassal is sold to a Vendee, the Vassal is the sole property of that Vendee for the duration of the arrangement. A Vendee will do with a Vassal as they wish, with impunity.'

201 did not always understand every concept arising in the manual. This particular section, however, made 201 feel unsure, even fearful, though she did not know why.

She placed the book next to her bed, wrapped herself up in the coverings and waited for sleep. The bland, piped music filtered through to her ears and she found herself drifting, clearing her mind of troubled thoughts and settling towards sleep.

6

That night she dreamed of a droning sound, a blaring, garish hum that hurt her ears and made her chest constrict alarmingly. She found herself panting, hunched over, hand on the rough, unfamiliar surface. She glanced up to find she was clinging to a tree, one of the trees that grew outside her window, the rough, pebbled surface chafing her palm. She felt the pulse entering her being, her heart beating faster, and faster. She knew she was done for but there was nothing more to be found by turning back. The ward zone was behind her now, and she knew she would not return, no matter what the consequence. 201 felt desperation coming off her body in waves as she turned to a rocky outcrop spreading before her, vast and desolate.

The suspension zone.

201 did not know the origin of this voice, but she felt it to be true. Somewhere, far beyond this 'suspension zone', was something new, something different, and she was certain, something better.

She felt herself move forward, standing tall, and pushing forwards, regardless of the palpitations within her chest. The pounding of her heart grew louder, and louder, as she felt the first spike shooting through her chest, explosions sounding in her ears. She jerked, chest arching without her consent. She pushed forward, eyes on the rocks and barren plains of the suspension zone. She jerked again, frozen, pinned to the spot, another buzzing shock reverberating through her chest and dissipating throughout her body. She could hear a distant screaming, not realizing it was coming from her own mouth. She slumped, curled in on herself, fingers clinging to the barren ground, and felt no more.

7

"Line check!" The Officer's voice rang out, jarring 201 from her contemplation. She straightened her shoulders and stood to attention. The Epsilon beauty pill from this morning remained lodged in her throat, tickling uncomfortably.

"Internees of Epsilon. We are gathered here to send our gratitude to Pinnacle Officer Wilcox and FERTS, for our daily provision and protection from those who would seek to strike against our Vassals, our Fighters and our Internees."

"We send our gratitude to Pinnacle Officer Wilcox and FERTS," the line replied, 201 calling out the words with enthusiasm.

"All Internees report to ration room before training commencement."

201 poked her head from the long line of faces, searching for 232. Her companion was in her usual place, four chambers to the right, filing through with the other Internees. 201 slowed her pace so 232 could catch up. 232's numbers glowed from her jumpsuit's panel insignia. 259232 23Y. 232 had been in Epsilon for longer than 201, her two years of training as a Fighter had made her strong, wiry muscles gently framing her lean form. Her dark brown hair swished

behind her as she walked, freckles standing out from her pleasing features. Her attractiveness rating was last recorded at 7.5, most likely due to her freckles and breaking muscle mass regulations while in Omega Circuit.

"Did you sneak off to the exercise room again last night?" 232 nudged 201's shoulder, grinning mischievously.

"Not this time," 201 muttered, distracted. "I need to lose muscle mass this time, not gain it. Got a negative appraisal for muscle mass."

"You need to make up your mind. Are you going to be a Fighter, like me, or are you going to be one of those fragile pretty things up in Omega?"

201 shook her head. "I don't know. I like fighting, I think I'm good at it."

"You are. Not as good as me, of course, but you could do well."

"I've only been training for a couple of months."

"You don't have many months left," 232 mused, flicking the numbers on 201's insignia. "Look, you're a 24Y now. Not long. That's what they say, anyway."

"I know. I can't decide. I don't want to be a Vassal, but I don't want to get hurt in the hall arena."

232 shook her head. "That is what happens in the arena. You might need to check your understanding of fighting next time." They seated themselves at the ration tables, shuffling down the metal seats until they reached the other Internees.

"But seriously, 201. You are a good Fighter, you know you are, I know you are. I just... I think you should maybe try to move up for promotion. Once you're hurt, that's the end of it for any chance of promotion. For me, I don't need to worry so much, but you could get back up without any trouble."

"I'd miss you, though. I don't know anyone else, really." 201 pushed her regulation food around on her metal tray, grimacing.

"I'd miss you too. But you need to do what is best for you. And it could be that maybe fighting isn't for you." 232 began to eat the regulation protein ration, wrinkling her nose in disapproval.

"What is the point? I don't even want to be sold to a Vendee. The idea frightens me."

A couple of curious Epsilon Internees turned to stare.

Internee 272 leaned in. "You should not be saying such things. Unless, of course, you want a demotion to Zeta Circuit." 232 inhaled sharply, giving 201 a warning look.

"What do you know of Zeta Circuit?" 201 shot back.

"222 was sent there last year. I knew her, her chambers were next to mine for a time."

"Why was she sent to Zeta?"

"She tried to run, the usual reason. They found her, got her back. It was the beacon that stopped her."

201 shook her head. "That cannot be true. They say nobody is promoted from Zeta, it's one way only. So, how did she tell you anything? How did you even see her?"

272 lowered her voice, glancing around the table at the various unconcerned faces, busy with eating and noisily discussing various fighting techniques and training routines.

"I saw her once, when I got lost coming back between the training and games hall, I forgot which floor it was I needed to find. She was in a caged room at the end of a long hall with all the other Zeta Internees, their jumpsuits were grey, that's how I knew who they were. I managed to speak to her, just for a moment, from between the bars."

"What did she say?" 201 whispered, lowering her voice to match 272's. 272 shifted closer, making sure to keep out of hearing distance from any Ration Officer that might be passing their little group.

"It was cold, so cold there. There were no fires to heat that part, the area where they were staying. It was hard to hear her above the other Zeta Internees. They were crying." 272 looked pained for a moment, then continued. "She looked so sick, I don't know if they get full rations. They all looked sick. She said to me, 'Don't ever come here. Make sure you tell the others. There is nothing here.' I had to leave before one of the Officers arrived. I could hear him coming down the hall."

"You never saw her after that?" 272 shook her head.

"I remembered the way, all the turns, all the doors and floors. I tried once, it was hard to take such a risk, but she wasn't there. The room was full of Zeta Internees, but I couldn't find her. I had to stop trying after that. She had warned me never to come again, so I stopped." 272 paused, looking blankly across the tables of the ration room.

"272 is right. We should not talk of this. It is not safe." 232 leaned in closer to 201's ear. "At least, not here. You must be careful of what you say, and who you say it to. You cannot trust, be careful not to trust." The last part was whispered, barely audible to 201's ear, let alone the surrounding Internees.

"I trust you," 201 whispered, darting her eyes to 232's.

232's blue eyes began to twinkle. "Yes, I trust you too. But no one else, understand?"

201 nodded, attempting to take a bite from one of the watery tasting squares of regulation protein.

8

Pinnacle Officer Wilcox sat at his desk, surrounded by dim light. He had shaved this night, face first, then his head, so as not to dull the blade. This was his regulation order, one he had devised for himself, and for his Officers. All activity could only run according to a predetermined order, anything else was chaos, much like the period succeeding the war.

The war had been a messy business. The technology was crude, in Wilcox's opinion, much of the damage caused by overuse of gunpowder and various other explosive materials. The planes that dropped these payloads were small, and less than powerful due to the rudimentary nature of the planes' engines. Had Wilcox been in command of the troops during these dark times, he would have spent his time on research, on technology, development and refinement of design to create a new breed of weapon, perhaps something that could be remotely discharged from a great distance away. Instead, the battles had been cumbersome, flying from township to township, systematically destroying as many structures as possible. The other side had been equally armed, so for each township destroyed by one, another was destroyed in retaliation. Soon came the time when there were so few resources such as fuel and metals, hampering the efforts of the ongoing battles. There were so few townspeople left, and comparatively fewer soldiers, that it became clear that the war could not go on. By that stage, there were no real groups remaining to claim victory, just a few stragglers with no direction, and nowhere to call home.

His thin mouth curled up in a smirk, insignia glowing in the muted glow of the lamp. He had achieved so much in his time, engineering and creating a new order, a solution to the chaos. But there was so much yet to accomplish, he told himself. This was no time to get complacent.

The plans spread before him were a source of constant frustration. The Implant Markers needed an upgrade. Many of the Officers were under the mistaken impression that the Implant Markers were somehow linked to the insignia on the Internees' uniforms. The fact was, the insignia were personally entered by hand, and mainly by Wilcox himself. Each Internee's Beth number was typed in and saved around the time of birth. All numbers began with 259 and ended with another three digit number, now in the two hundreds. The number of Internees was actually around a few hundred. There had been perhaps a few hundred that had come before, all expired now. And there would be new Internees, but the process of birthing was a maddeningly slow one, the whole process was too damn slow for Wilcox's liking.

The fundamental problem, Wilcox decided, was the ratio of Officers to Internees. There were only fifty or so, with twenty Operators to take care of the running of the Epsilon Games, surveillance and rations duty. Various Internees were scheduled for duties, taking up the slack from the shortfall in personnel. There simply weren't enough to go around. Weapons were in short supply, but the Internees were subservient, and dutiful, just as he had engineered them. The 'beauty pill' took care of unwanted birthing, and it had the added bonus of taming the nature of the Internees, making them docile. Unfortunately, it was only effective on some of the Internees, others were entirely unaffected, making them somewhat more difficult to control. Hormones, always problems with the hormones, so unpredictable, so... Chaotic. Still, the threat of Zeta Circuit and the Kappa work duties kept the majority in line.

A knock sounded at the door.

"Come." Wilcox smoothed the plans on the desk, fixing the ends in place with heavy weights made from quartz, a resource plentiful in the surrounding territories. What he most needed was a source of more diverse metals, and skilled labor, perhaps even a facility in which to forge them.

Officer Cerberus stood in the doorway, squinting in his usual manner.

"Five more recommendations for Zeta, Sir."

"Show me."

Cerberus handed over the scrawled list of numbers. Wilcox brought each up on the Beth Register, pleasing faces staring out from the screen.

"This one?"

"Attempted escape, brought back by the beacon."

"And this one?"

"Bit an Officer. This one has shown aptitude in the Games Ring, however this Internee prefers to fight both in and out of the ring."

Wilcox brought up the next face on the screen.

"Self harm. Scars." Wilcox's mouth twitched downwards in disdain.

The next face appeared, hopeful eyes pleading through the screen.

"This one... Will not eat. This has gone on for many months. This Internee will be expired before long, it's unpleasant for the Officers, there have been many complaints."

The final face flickered on the screen, power draining to a trickle from the nightly generators. Wilcox sighed, clenching his fist on the table.

"The panels? How did they charge today?"

"Not so well, this weather has not been conducive for optimum charge. Also, the panels are very old. We can only hope to repair them." The power kicked back in, illuminating the screen once more.

"This will not do, you must make sure they run at optimum efficiency."

"Yes, Sir."

"Well?" Wilcox waved a hand in the general direction of the screen.

"This one doesn't speak. Hasn't spoken since three months ago."

Wilcox looked at him expectantly.

"I asked around. Officer Seph chose her sometime around that time, said she wasn't very good."

"And that's it? She doesn't speak?"

"That's it."

"Send all to Zeta except the last one. We don't need them to speak, we need them to serve. It would be preferable if more were like this one." He tapped the screen with the back of his knuckles.

"Yes Sir."

"That will be all." He waved his hand towards the door, returning to his plans. The insignia needed an upgrade, he needed to connect them somehow with the Implant Markers. The Y numbers were set around the time of birth, give or take a few days, and from that point on, the insignia was basically a simple chronograph, much like a timepiece, increasing in number each 365 days, from zero to twenty-six.

Wilcox banged the table in frustration, pushing the plans to the side. The intermittent Ward Beacon used too much power as it was, it would be preferable to have the ability to control each Internee directly through the Implant Markers, rather than using a rudimentary system of sound and electricity. The body scanning device, a relic left over from before the war, could only be used for one to two minutes at a time, lest it drained the remaining power to the entire facility. However, the piped music was a more successful experiment, using subliminal theta technology to induce sleep waves. It was a simple system, a phonograph, a single classical record, the only music he could find. It was bland, inoffensive, precisely what had been required for his purposes. The regular, rhythmic beeping of the five cycles per second was created by an makeshift automated Morse code transmitter. So far, the experiment had been effective for coercing sleep in the Internee population.

Wilcox scrolled through the Beth Register again, one of his more pleasurable activities, settling on one with big blue eyes and auburn hair.

Yes, this one would do. This one would do nicely.

He flipped off his screen.

"Guard Officer!"

9

The training room was longer than it was wide, various weapons lining the walls. 201 passed the row of weapons, gleaming and polished to a modest shine. None of these weapons were really clean, 201 noticed.

Sometimes it was a trace of blood, a speck, a stray hair of red or blonde, a dull brown stain near the hilt where the blood would never fully be removed.

232 rushed past her, hair swishing in a long plait down her back as she lunged for the sword rack.

"Ha! Mine!" she cried, gripping a straight sword with a flat, broad blade.

"232, I would never steal your sword. It is your weapon of choice. You know I would never let anyone else take it either, at least for training drills."

"That is right, because if anyone did..." She reared back, unsheathing and swirling the sword gracefully. "They would never make that mistake again! I would expire them, swiftly!" 232 doubled back, arcing the blade around her head. "They must learn to fear..."

"232!" She froze, standing to attention. "What are you doing?"

232 turned to face Reno, the High Training Room Officer. His uniform was sleek black, thin leather armour detailing his chest and torso. He always stood

straight, large shoulders squared, his shaved head catching the light.

"I said, what are you doing?"

"I was practising?" 232 ventured.

"No, 232. You were fooling around. A wonderful way to get oneself killed. A spatha is not to be toyed with."

"But I had full control, I knew where my sword was placed at all times."

Reno was silent, unmoving. The silence drew out for a little longer than expected and 201 stepped back, uncomfortable. Reno caught her eye for a moment, then moved his head, almost imperceptibly to fix on 232.

"Then why, perhaps you can answer this, was the sword unsheathed?" he spat the words out venomously, voice raising in intensity. A couple of Epsilon trainees faltered in their warm-up routine, turning to peer at 232.

"I thought..."

"No, 232. You did not think. That is the problem. The protective sheath is there for a reason. It is not just to protect you, it is to protect your fellow Epsilon trainees! This is a serious matter. You can get expired, quite easily I might add. This makes no difference to me one way or the other. I see it so often, you see, Fighters are expired all the time, but I would wager that it might matter to you. Do not make me regret my decision to consider your promotion to Fighter."

232 hung her head, studying the floor intently as other Epsilon trainees looked on.

"Ten laps of the training room and forty push ups. Now. Do it!"

232 loped off in a slow jog, shaking her head.

"Faster 232. No dragging your feet!"

Reno shifted his eyes back to 201.

"You. Have you chosen your weapon?"

201 scanned the rows, finding her chosen sword, the one that had always felt most comfortable in her hand.

"This one." She held it up, making sure the transparent sheath protector remained intact.

"Hmm. Fine choice." He took it from her hand, raising it to the light and turning it to the side so the blade glinted with each movement. "A bastard sword. You can use this weapon with one hand, but also two, should you need that kind of flexibility. In the old times, they were known as 'hand and a half swords', lighter than their two-handed counterparts. Someone like you needs a sword light enough to wield, but strong enough to do damage. Your strength alone perhaps. would not be enough. Maybe, with further training. But with this..." he mused, flipping it over and handing it back, hilt first. "Practice defensive drills. You cannot attack without first being able to defend. Now. Do it!"

201 turned her back to the wall, standing in ready position. She imagined her opponent, large and menacing as she swung towards her. 201 dropped to one knee, sword deftly raised to block the imaginary blow. She could almost see her opponent, vulnerable, unguarded at this moment. She smiled secretly to

herself, swinging the blade in an arc, cutting her phantom opponent off at the knees.

"201! Do you not understand the meaning of the word 'defensive'! One more trick like that one and you'll be joining 232." 201 glanced over at 232, hunched over, dripping with sweat, crouching and attempting to get in position for yet another bout of push ups.

He strode behind 201, dipping his head and lowering his voice so only she could hear. "You're dead, by the way. Your opponent took the opportunity while your sword was lowered to cut you in half. You cannot afford yourself one reckless moment, for that is all you will get." He strode off to attend to another Epsilon trainee, wielding her cutlass in a menacing fashion.

201 breathed in sharply and took to her drills with renewed focus. She imagined her opponent once more, sword piercing directly towards her chest. She swung the sword in an arc, curtailing any unnecessary effort at theatrics. She replicated the move, repeating and repeating until she found she could do it without effort.

"Good, 201. Keep it up." Reno strode by, heading for a group of Epsilon trainees who had decided to scuffle instead of drill.

After training, 201 sat on the bench seats lining the farthest wall, fastening her boots under her Epsilon regulation red jumpsuit.

Reno stood before her, posture alert, arms resting by his sides.

"201, I have come to the decision that I cannot promote you to Fighter. Not yet. You have too much to learn. One thing I will say is this. You are a natural Fighter, a good one. But most certainly not one of the best. And you will be crushed if you try to challenge any of the foremost Fighters skilled through combat in the Epsilon Games Ring."

201 looked up at Reno, untucking the cuff of her jumpsuit from inside her boots. She tried to hide her disappointment but judging by the look on Reno's face, she had not succeeded.

"But you have something the others do not. The Fighters in rotation for the Games Circuit are made to fight, that is their way. But you have something else. You have this." He pressed his finger firmly against her forehead, pressing again to make his point. "I did not need to read your intelligence rating to know this. You must know when to fight, and when not to fight."

201 studied his face, leaning her back against the wall.

"So you have this. Use it. This is all I will say to you." Reno was walking away before she had time to reply. Her forehead carried the press of his finger long after he was gone.

10

The following morning, the training room was filled with excitement, chatters echoing from each of the far corners of the room. The fight trainees gathered, eagerly anticipating the monthly Fighter selection through the Epsilon Chance Wheel. The wheel could assign one of the nominated fight trainees to the Epsilon Games Ring, it could promote any Epsilon Internee to the highest status of Alpha Field, but it could also relegate any Epsilon Internee to the scrapheap of Zeta Circuit.

Reno stood stoically, arms placed behind his back, legs slightly apart. He looked on, his blank face betraying nothing as Games Operator Farrenlowe stood before the Epsilon Wheel of Chance. The wheel was predominantly painted in Epsilon red, interspersed with blue, grey and green. He gestured dramatically at the gathered Epsilon fight trainees, cloak waving wildly as his voice roared through the training room.

"Before we begin, we will send our gratitude to Pinnacle Officer Wilcox and FERTS, for our daily provision and protection from those who would seek to strike against our Vassals, our Fighters and our Internees."

"We send our gratitude to Pinnacle Officer Wilcox and FERTS," the trainees replied somberly.

"Epsilon fight trainees. Potential Epsilon Fighters. Today may be the luckiest day of all. For today is the day we find out..." He paused for dramatic effect. "Who..."

"Will be the next Epsilon Fighters!" the trainees called back in unison. 201 looked around, puzzled. 232 winked at her.

"I forgot it's your first time," she whispered. "You'll get used to it."

"So, are you ready to make High Training Room Officer Reno proud?"

The trainees yelled and whistled.

"Are you ready to make Pinnacle Officer Wilcox proud?"

The trainees whooped and applauded.

"Are you ready to join the champions in the Epsilon Fight Ring?"

The training room exploded in cheers and shouts. 201 clapped enthusiastically, smiling over at 232.

He placed his hand in a small metal bucket, rummaging around.

"285!" He produced the selected number triumphantly, displaying it so all could see.

The Internees fell into silence. 285 shifted her stance, shrugging at her fellow trainees, eyes forward.

"Spin the wheel and let chance decide!" The Beta Internee, dressed immaculately in her white jumpsuit, smiled at the trainees, spinning the wheel with a flourish.

The wheel spun, ticking as it went. The trainees were silent, mesmerized by the rhythm. 201 could barely read the markings as they merged into one brownish shade, ticking and clicking.

Tick.

Fight

Click.

Fight

Tick.

Zeta Circuit

Click.

Fight

Click.

Alpha Field

Click...

Fight

The trainees cheered, hoisting 285 above them, her green eyes both startled and triumphant, light wispy brown hair bouncing with excitement.

"Ah... but what is a Fighter without..."

"A weapon!" the crowd shot back, 285 cheering heartily from her elevated perch.

The Beta Internee strode to a second wheel, the segments decked out in red and green. She gave it a good shove, the wheel taking off at a frantic pace.

Click.

bastard sword

Tick.

shotel

Click.

scimitar

Tick.

spatha

Click.

trident

285 cheered, the trident being her favored weapon, her first choice.

"285 is truly lucky," 232 remarked. "I will cheer for her tomorrow night. I am on water duty."

"I will hear the fight from the weapons room. Perhaps I will cheer silently, it is not regulation to make undue noise on weapons duty." The other two Fighters were chosen with much excitement, the wheel spinning and twirling, clicking and ticking.

That night, 201's sleep was disturbed by a wheel that wouldn't stop spinning, no matter how long it ran. The ticking was maddening, drowning out the soothing music piping through to her bed. The red and grey wheel spun in a loop, every word visible, instead of slowing it began spinning faster and faster, louder and louder.

Click.

Expired

Tick.

Expired

Click.

Expired

Tick.

Expired

Tick.

Expired

Tick. Click. Tick.

11

"All Fighters report to Games Circuit. All fight trainees to games supply. Menial internees report to designated posts"

201 hurried through the gathered Epsilon Internees and made her way to the weapons store room. She was alone this night, often there would be another Epsilon Internee on weapons duty to accompany her for the duration.

She sighed, picking up the trident, polishing the points with a foul smelling oil, careful to avoid the grips. Her hands were encased in protective mail gloves, ensuring she would not slip and earn herself a scar for her troubles.

She laid out the trident on the ready table, providing easy access for the fight attendees to carry the weapons into the Epsilon Games Ring.

Next, she selected a spatha, deftly slicking the blade with her stale-smelling cleaning rag. The spatha bore dents in its handle, this was not 232's chosen weapon, she noted. The wood of the hilt was stained a dark brown, the tang of old blood assaulting her nostrils.

A dull cheer broke out from the Games Ring, both jarring and muted. It jolted 201, having worked many nights in the weapons store room, she had never grown accustomed to the violent cries snaking their way down the hall.

She huffed out a shaky breath, laying down the spatha next to the trident. She selected a scimitar next, then a bastard sword that looked deceptively like her chosen weapon. A darker wood on the hilt was the only telling sign that her own sword was not yet in play. She selected another spatha, three more scimitars, a shotel and another trident. Another roar erupted from the Games Ring as the fights were opened and the games officially commenced. She could hear Games Operator Farrenlowe's familiar voice booming through the halls, goading the crowd into a frenzy.

"201! Where are the weapons?" 207 burst into the room, flustered, eyes darting around.

"On the ready table, where they always are." 201 motioned to the table as 207 hurriedly gathered up a trident, a scimitar, the shotel and a spatha.

"Hey 207?"

207 turned, her copper hair flying, her blue eyes animated, attempting to cling onto the weapons with her heavy mail gloves.

"Yes?"

"Wish 285 good fortune for her fight."

207's distracted grimace softened, relaxing into a smile.

"Yes, of course, I will do that. Thanks, 201."

201 smiled, perching herself on the ready table, listening to the cries of the crowd rising and falling,

the hollow jubilance stabbing at her senses. Head bowed, she swung her legs forwards, then backwards, forwards then backwards, feet rising and falling from her field of vision.

The gong sounded down the hall, the signal that fighting had commenced. Another cheer welled up before trailing into a dull chatter. The clash of steel on steel caused the hairs on 201's arms to rise all at once, as if pulled by strings. She could almost see the fight, 285's face enlivened by the thrill of battle. She could not picture the opponent, only a vague sense of her abilities filtered through her consciousness. 285's opponent was experienced and formidable, a good match. However, almost immediately, she could feel the inequality of the fight once it was underway. The opponent was cunning, easily trumping 285's open, straightforward nature. 201 began to feel a little sick.

Another clash of steel and a scream rang out, followed by a heavy silence. 201 held her breath, waiting for something, anything to break the tension. She heard a cough, then an exultant cheer rose up from the Games Ring, filtering down the hall, trickling into the confines of the weapons room. The gong sounded out and the clink of cider mugs grew louder, interspersed with shouts and raucous babble.

The next time she saw 207, her familiar cheerful features were unrecognizable underneath the mask of shock. 201 didn't need to ask, and instead chose not to speak at all. The sounds of mail and steel shuffled towards her, jangling erratically.

207 stepped forward, shaking fingers handing over the trident, the tips lightly dusted with flecks of blood and a few blonde hairs. The handle, however, was stained a bright red, the blood soaked deeply through to the heart of the wood.

12

201 curled in bed, trying to put all thoughts of 285 out of her head. She attempted to distract herself by reading the seduction manual once more, the illustrations within making her feel uncomfortable, and more than a little sick.

'A Vassal must succumb to the advances of the Vendee. If a Vassal refuses a Vendees advances, the Vendee has authorization to take by force. A Vassal must try to relax, as a tense Vassal will find it disagreeable as the coupling commences.'

201 closed the book, disgusted by the crude illustrations and the thought of being charged with such an undertaking. She tossed the book to the side, pulling the covers around her, the piped music seeping into her being, lulling her to oblivion.

That night 201 dreamed of earth, and fresh grasses, much like the ones that grew outside her window, far from reach. She saw boots tramping, their points piercing her field of vision, her gaze tilted down to behold only the earth and the grass beneath her. The sounds of running water filled her ears. Narrowing her gaze, her boots looked strange, as if her feet were too big or too small, it was difficult to tell. She was running, unfamiliar sounds crunching underfoot as she heard her own breathing, panting, wheezing. The boots poked into her vision once more and it was only then she saw they were splattered with blood.

I am free. I am free. I am free.

She stopped, her vision swinging around to take in a large, wondrous expanse of earth, with grasses, trees and shrubs. She approached the rushing sound, washing her hands in the running waters, the coolness seeping into her being.

Suddenly she heard a snort. It was thick, and low. It seemed to echo in the space surrounding her. Fear prickled and itched at her temples, sweat gathering and trickling down behind her ear. A resonant, whining bellow erupted behind her and she fell to her knees, turning her head, afraid of what she might see there.

I am not alone. I am not alone. I am not alone.

13

"Line Check!"

"Internees of Epsilon. We will send our gratitude to Pinnacle Officer Wilcox and FERTS, for our daily provision and protection from those who would seek to strike against our Vassals, our Fighters and our Internees."

"We send our gratitude to Pinnacle Officer Wilcox and FERTS," the line replied.

201 peered down the line of Internees, spotting 232. 232's eyes were cast downwards, it was clear she had not slept well, or perhaps not at all.

201 slowed her pace to the ration room, allowing 232 to catch up. 232 took more time than usual this morning, moving at a sluggish rate.

"Everyone's talking about it already."

"I know. I heard."

"I was there 201. I saw her fall. She was pierced through the chest. There was a lot of blood." 232's face was pale, eyes trained elsewhere, seeing, remembering.

"Do you still want to fight?" 201 asked, studying 232's tired features.

"Of course. It is not the first time I have seen a Fighter fall, and it will not be the last. Next month, I believe I will nominated for the wheel. Reno thinks I'm ready, and he would not let a novice enter the Games Ring."

"He doesn't think I'm close to being a Fighter yet. Perhaps a few more months of training."

"We'll see."

"She expired proud, as a true Fighter." 232 hardened her features, staring ahead.

201 nodded, following 232 into the ration hall.

"Do you ever wonder about it? About why we must do this, why we must be Vassals, or Fighters? I mean, supposing there were no Games? Do you ever wonder if one day, we could be something else? What it would be like, perhaps, to be... free from this?"

232 swung around, eyes flashing with tears.

"Do not say such things! Not those words, not now. 285 expired a true Fighter, proud and strong. We must venerate the memory of her contribution, you must not degrade her achievements again. You will speak no more of this."

232 pushed forward into the crowd of Epsilon Internees, choosing a seat on the bench near another group of fight trainees. 201 sunk to her usual spot, an unfamiliar Internee to her left perched in the spot typically saved for 232.

14

That evening, 201 could not sleep. Her disagreement with 232 played on her mind. She oscillated from being furious at 232 for not listening to her point of view, and feeling sorrowful for interfering with the quiet veneration of 285's achievements.

But what has 285 achieved, other than expiration?

Her mind wandered, taking her to far off places, and people she did not recognize or understand. There was warmth, and pleasant scents, and most wonderfully, the sparkling sound of true, unbridled laughter.

Somewhere, there is more than this. I must find it.

Another voice trailed into her thoughts, familiar and soothing, wrapping around her mind and lilting her to sleep.

One day, I believe we, all of us, will be free.

15

"Line Check!"

The Officer recited the FERTS Requital, pausing for the response from the line.

"We send our gratitude to Pinnacle Officer Wilcox and FERTS," came the murmured reply.

201 peered down the row to pick 232 out of the Internees, standing to attention. For the past few weeks, 232 had refused meet 201's eyes, no matter how forcefully 201 tried to catch her attention. 232 did not catch up to match her footsteps, nor did she sit at the ration bench in her usual spot.

201 poked at the regulation protein, dissecting it into pieces and pushing them around her plate. She had missed her beauty pill most days this week, too distracted by the animosity between her and 232. She wanted to scream, to apologize, to have 232 apologize to her for the disagreement. She fought the urge to push past the other Internees and confront 232, to do something to fix things back to the way they were before. But she did not move, and the conversations continued, the murmured veneration of 285, the results of the fight, anticipation for the next shot at the Epsilon Chance Wheel.

Suddenly, her stomach clenched violently and she lurched forward, hugging herself tightly.

The Internee on her left, 278, reached out and gripped 201's shoulder.

"Uh, 201, is it? Are you alright?"

201 tried to speak, but her words were swallowed by another bout of pain.

"Come, 201, I will take you back to your chambers. You are not well. You do not want Reno to get word of this or he will never let you fight. Come on."

201 attempted to stand straight but the pain was too intense. She settled for bending down, hunched over as 278 guided her back through the walkway to her chambers.

"Here, lie down. I will get you some water."

201 felt a dull snap deep within her and suddenly there was wetness trickling from between her legs. 201 went cold with fear. She pressed her legs together tightly, attempting to stop the flow.

What is happening to me? Am I expiring?

278 handed her the water, oblivious to the blood seeping through the inner seams of 201's jumpsuit.

"Thank you."

"Oh, I'm glad you can talk. I was starting to wonder."

"Thank you for helping me. I think I just need to lie down. It seemed the rations did not agree with me today."

278 nodded. "Don't worry, the rations don't agree with me on any day."

201 attempted to smile, resulting in a half-grimace.

"I will leave you to rest now. It seems you will miss the Fighter selection this day."

"Perhaps that is just as well. I would do no good in the Games Ring as I am right now. Again, thank you. It was kind of you to help."

"Wish me good fortune then, I am up for selection tonight."

"Good fortune to you. I hope you are successful."

278 left with quick strides, the door sucking shut behind her.

201 leapt from the bed as soon as 278 was out of view. She rushed to the bathroom, stripping off her clothes to find that yes, she was indeed bleeding. Terrified, she showered briskly, trying to clean all traces of blood from her body. She wrapped herself in a towel, fastening it in a knot like an undergarment. She draped herself in another towel and filled the bath with cold, not hot water. Her time in the weapons room had taught her that cold water was the only thing that could remove blood from cloth. Cold water, plenty of soap and time to soak. Exhausted, she dragged herself back to her bed, clutching at her aching belly and curling in a ball, wrapping the coverings around her until she began to feel warm. As the pain ebbed away and the tension finally drained from her body, 201 slept.

16

Her body ached and she was soaked with sweat. 201 had overslept and missed morning line check. A cursory glance into her chambers was all she received from the Officer on duty, her soiled clothing tucked inside the bathroom, covered in towels. As the Officer left, she wrenched herself from the bed and frantically washed all traces of blood from her jumpsuit, throwing it in the washing slot.

She had taken her beauty pill last night, and another in the morning. Miraculously, the bleeding had slowed and finally in the early afternoon it had stopped altogether. She washed each towel until each was scrupulously clean, throwing them unceremoniously through the washing slot. She showered again, ignoring regulation order and staggered out of the shower, newly exhausted. She dried herself with a fresh towel and curled up once more, shivering into a disturbed sleep.

The wheel was spinning once more, every word standing out in bright clear letters, it clicked along, speeding up as it went. The middle of the wheel was unmoving, Games Operator Farrenlowe's shiny face laughing uproariously as the wheel spun around his bodiless head.

Click.
Expired
Tick.
Expired
Click.
Expired
Tick.
Expired
Tick.
Expired
Ticka. Clicka. Tick.

17

Pinnacle Officer Wilcox sat alone in his study, perusing the daily reports from his Officers. Tonight was the monthly games night hosted in his honor for the Epsilon Games. Pinnacle Officer Wilcox never attended the fights in the Games Ring, he preferred to leave that to his Officers. He smiled to himself, silently congratulating his own ingenuity. To some, the Epsilon Games was a spectacle, an inconsequential diversion, a break in the daily routine to loosen up and enjoy the show. What they did not understand was the design. This was a microcosm of what society should be, what he held as the ideal of how to control, to create order out of chaos.

The Officers were much like the Resident Citizens, they had simple needs that must be fulfilled. Fundamentally, they needed certainty. There would be no fighting over Vassals and Internees. If an Officer wanted to take an Internee, it mattered not, because the next night another Officer could take her for himself. The primitive territorial demarcation over the opposite sex was an archaic notion to be left in the dark days, the days before the war. The Officers' natural thirst for blood was slaked by the monthly fights, and by removing the main catalysts for such altercations between Officers, it created a neatness, an order that had not been experienced before now. The system, of course, was not perfect. There was the odd scuffle over a bet, or allocation of drinks, but largely, the structure was upheld in relative decorum. It would take time, of course, he was under no illusions about this fact. The main objective however, was peace. Through the grace and order at FERTS, he would create peace, through a system of basic needs fulfilment, following strict regulation. This was an achievable ideal, a contentment simply accomplished through the joy of collectively pursuing a common goal for the betterment not only for the population at FERTS, but for the benefit of all townships in the wider Forkstream Territories.

18

"All Fighters report to Games Circuit. All fight trainees to secondary games supply. All menial Internees report to designated posts."

201 was on water duty for her first Games Circuit attendance. She had scurried along the halls, unsure of where to go after missing both line check and rations for the last day and a half. She had been posted for weapons room cleaning duty so many times, spending her evenings polishing and oiling blades. So many nights spent removing the blood, hair and other debris left over from the bloodshed in the Games Ring. The smell had sickened her, sweet but cloying with a metallic tang that never seemed to leave the airless storehouse. Tonight, however, was the first night she had seen the hall arena itself.

She worked quickly to fill the water containers, and kept them close to the Fighter's blocks should the Fighters get thirsty. It seemed to be a straightforward duty, much simpler than her weapons room routine. She wondered why there were not more Epsilon Internees clamoring for simple tasks such as this.

The hall arena was large, much larger than the viewing, instruction and ration rooms. Rows and rows of smooth metal seats surrounded the walls, sloping down in tiers to enclose the Epsilon Games Ring. The circular ring was plain, covered with piles of fragrant wood shavings, surrounded by sharpened wire. The Officers had begun to file in, a sea of dispassionate faces, dressed in dark suits, accepting drinks from her fellow Epsilon Internees. This was the night the Officers received an opportunity to unwind and play. This was a night for Officers to be entertained, to bet and to drink. She spotted 205, her blonde hair hanging loosely below her shoulders. She was well-muscled, arms hinting at a wiry toughness and the coiled sprightliness that lay beneath her unassuming exterior. 201 supposed she was an unlikely candidate for promotion to Omega based on muscle mass alone. Her face was sharp with a pointed nose and keen eyes. She had received an attractiveness rating of 7.2 though 201 could not see what had prompted such a rating. 201 thought that most all the Internees were attractive in some way or another, but she supposed that she was not in charge of ratings, so her opinions were irrelevant.

Internees at Beta and Omega were encouraged to appraise each other, offering criticism and maintaining a culture of rivalry and competition. 201 had no desire to participate in such activities. It seemed so pointless, to focus all one's attention on whether 257 had splits at the end of her hair, or whether 243 had dry cheeks. What did it matter? They were to be sold as Vassals or work in Kappa or participate in the games in Epsilon. What was it to her if another Internee had dirt under her nails. 201 did not enjoy being appraised, why should the other Internees?

She scanned the crowd once more, checking for 232. Since she had missed ration room this evening, 201 had no means of finding out where she could be. 201 smiled to herself. 232 was quiet, but when she talked, she was mildly amusing, and sarcastic, much like 201 herself. 201 missed her freckles, and the way her blue eyes sparkled when she talked. 201 wanted desperately to speak to her companion once more, to apologize, to say something to break this tension between them.

Games Operator Farrenlowe entered the ring, two Epsilon Internees holding apart the sharpened wire with strong mail gloves, built for withstanding the barbs. His coat was long, black on the outside and burgundy lined, displaying the FERTS games insignia around his neck. The symbol displayed a sword crossing a spear, mounted on a shield. The silver insignia glowed and glittered under the too-warm lights of the Epsilon Games Ring.

"Welcome, esteemed Officers to the monthly routine Epsilon Battle!" A loud cheer rose up from the crowd, drinks splashing noisily on the shavings below. Rows of Officers elbowed and jostled, handing over their wagers eagerly to the hosting Epsilon pledge-takers.

"Will you please stand for the FERTS Requital." The Officers stood, cider mugs held high in the air.

"Esteemed Officers, Fighters of Epsilon, menial Internees. We now send our gratitude to Pinnacle

Officer Wilcox and FERTS, for our daily provision and protection from those who would seek to strike against our Vassals, our Fighters and our Internees."

"We send our gratitude to Pinnacle Officer Wilcox and FERTS," came the enthusiastic reply.

"As you know we have a Beth for ALL occasions." His voice boomed throughout the hall arena as some of the attending Officers laughed. Sharp, barking sounds rang out from behind 201, as she spied the fighting creatures in their crates. One of the dogs snarled, a thin stream of drool escaping over its unnaturally sharpened teeth. From what she had heard from her fellow menial Internees, the fighting creatures were fodder in between fights, enough to keep the Officers occupied while the new Fighters prepared for their next challenge.

"And we know how you all love to watch the blue eyed ones cry, so without further ado, she's bad, she's a master with the spatha, a first-timer tonight, our very own Beth 259232!"

No.

201 looked up just in time to see 232, dressed in full Fighter regalia, stepping deftly between the wires and into the ring. The shavings puffed up under her feet, sparkling as they fell like rain under the heavy lights. Her feet, sheathed in leather criss-cross bindings, her leather skirt, short and barely able to conceal anything important. Her breastplate, also leather, was bound tightly around her torso, muscles standing out in stark relief, catching the light with her dark brown hair, tied loosely in a plait that hung

down her back, swishing from side to side. Her wide blue eyes appeared to twinkle underneath the lights, a thin sheen of sweat covering her face. 201 had never seen her look so powerful, so strong, yet so vulnerable. The Fighter's attendants handed over a shield and sword between the wires, the shield catching for a moment on the barbs as she fastened them both in position, glancing around the ring for signs of what was to come.

"And the challenger... You know her, I know her." More cheers and whistles from the crowd. "She's the meanest one, the biggest, the best, the red head, she's fiery, she's feisty, and she wants blood. It's Beth 259299!"

The crowd roared with appreciation, splashes from the Officers' cider mugs spraying over 201's shoulders. She shivered, brushing off the droplets. As she raised her eyes to the ring, she caught 299's eye. She was tall, much taller than most of the Internees 201 had ever seen. Her broad back rippled with muscles, her leather armour ridiculously small on her huge frame. 299's hair fanned out high and proud around her head, glowing bright red under the lights, her dark green eyes momentarily fixed on 201, snarling her features into a smirk. A prickle of fear ran through 201. She looked over at 232, who was standing her ground, eyes fixed on 299, chin raised.

Get out 232. Getoutgetoutgetout!

201 could not stop the torrent of words running through her mind. 232 caught her eye and faltered, just for a brief moment. 201 tried to steel her features

into a supportive nod. She tried to convey a message of support, something to let 232 know she was not alone.

Ok. It's ok. You can do this.

Judging by 232's reaction, it seemed to have the desired effect.

299 bent down in a practised manner, gripping the gleaming scimitar and shield provided by the Fighter attendants. She twirled the scimitar, its curved blade flashing along with the white of her teeth as she gnashed at 232.

232, to her credit, did not flinch. She had been trained well, knew not to be intimidated by the posturing of her formidable opponent.

"It begins!" the Games Operator called to the crowd, two menial Internees sounding out the gongs for the fight to commence.

299 roared, squaring her shoulders and circling 232. 232 stood firm, eyes darting left and right, gripping her sword tightly.

In a flash the scimitar swung, seemingly out of nowhere, glancing 232's arm in a thin jagged line, blood flicking deftly from the blade. 232 flinched, looking up at 299's broad smiling features. 299 winked and blew her a kiss.

"That was nothing, whelp."

A scar. No chance of promotion now. No going back to Omega, not anymore.

232 faked to the right, then swung her sword to the left but it was too slow, merely scraping against 299's thigh, drawing a trickle of blood. 299 smiled, a

hungry smile full of teeth, and brought her hand to her thigh, sweeping it up into her mouth and licking her finger, raising an eyebrow. The crowd reached a crescendo, cheering her on.

232 took the chance while 299 was playing up to the crowd to kick her leg out, knocking 299 off balance. 299 went down hard with a curse as 232 loomed over her, ready to strike. But then something unexpected happened. 232's sword was coming down on 299 towards her midsection, but 299's scimitar flicked upwards, under 232's arm. The crowd screamed and roared as 232's arm fell to the floor in a puff of shavings, blood sticking to the wisps of wood dust, spattering in a star shaped pattern, rivulets running under the shavings to the floor below.

Before she knew it, 201 was at the Fighter's block with 232's slumped form, her trembling hands passing the water container to the Fighter's attendants.

"232! 232! Look at me." 201 was frantic, shouting her friend's name. 232 looked up with a dazed expression, her eyes clouded. A slow smile took over her face as she reached out her right arm to touch 201's face.

"201." She sighed, running a finger down 201's nose. "You have been good to me. I will remember you."

"I'm sorry, I'm sorry... 232..."

"Shh. I know, I know. I must finish the fight." She stumbled to her feet, the flesh of her left shoulder flapping alarmingly as she turned to face the ring.

"It continues!" The menial attendants rang out the gongs as 299 rose to her full height, scimitar twirling in a slow, rhythmic figure eight.

232 stood to address the crowd, chin jutted out in defiance. She spoke with a quiet strength, her voice reverberating throughout the hall arena. "One day, there will be no FERTS, no games. One day, I believe we, all of us, will be free." She caught 201's eye, gaze holding for a moment, features softening as she spoke without words, mouth curving in a hopeful smile. The crowd fell silent, confused murmurs drifting into the ring. She raised her sword above her head and with a cry, lunged to face 299's swirling scimitar. 232 caught 299's side with the sword, earning a cry from her opponent. Another swipe left a nasty gash on 299's thigh. Her third swipe, aimed at 299's chest fell short as the scimitar flew towards 232, swiping and swirling.

232's head fell to the floor with a heavy crash. Her eyes still open, stared into 201's. Her body teetered for a moment, shuddering to its knees and flopping backwards into a cloud of shavings. Frozen in place, the screams of the crowd and the money changing hands, the shouts for more drink, the lights flashing and the gongs signaling the end of the fight, 201 stared into the face of her friend. Her eyes seemed to soften once more, her hard edges disappearing into a quiet, contented smile.

19

201 shivered through the night, the maddeningly soothing music jarring her nerves. She flung off the covers, scrubbing her face clean of tears as she paced, muttering to herself. The seduction manual lay in its fallen position on the floor, pages splayed obscenely, mocking her.

She felt the energy building up within her, heart racing. She felt the need to do something, anything to burn off the discomfort. She could not sneak off to the exercise room, the weights were too tempting. She needed to be sharp, and she needed to be ready. She didn't quite know when she would need this, just that she must be perpetually ready. She narrowed her thoughts to constructing a training regime.

First she went through a series of stretches, making sure to maintain and increase flexibility in her arms, legs, without neglecting her ankles, wrists and back. She stretched and folded herself on the floor, raising on her toes, arms outstretched, only to drop back on the floor and do it all again. She ran drills, gripping the door frame between her bedchamber and the bathroom, hoisting herself into the air and back down again until her vision blurred with sweat. She jogged the perimeter of her bedchamber until her legs grew weary. She flung open the door to the bathroom, heading into the shower, forgoing the regulation bathing to just wash herself and be out of there in the quickest amount of time possible. She dried off and wrapped on her robe, sinking into her bed, hoping that she was too exhausted to cry. She was wrong. The sobs hacked out of her as she curled her fist in the sheets, slamming her hand on the bed in frustration.

Finally the tears slowed to a trickle and she sank into the bed, breathing shakily.

201 tried desperately to settle, the tears merging into the channels already forged on her cheeks.

Every time she closed her eyes, 232's eyes stared back at her, a halo of shavings surrounding her, dancing and falling under lights.

20

That night the unwelcome intrusion of dreams came once more to 201.

She was still, trapped upright in a room, stone, with no windows, no light. Her body was pressed against others, so tightly that she could not read their insignia. The room was mostly silent, which disturbed 201 most of all. A tiny cry started up from a short distance behind her, thin and piercing, smothered by a deeper voice, whispering soothing sounds.

There are little ones here.

201 tried to move, but found she could not dislodge her arms, nor could she move her legs. She turned her head to the side, twisting it around, straining to see, but there was only a flat, inky blackness on all sides. She felt the insistent press of the bodies around her, all trying to wriggle free, to change direction, to escape. She breathed the scent of the others, the sharp tang of sweat and fear rising up to her face, swirling around her, settling in her hair.

Suddenly the air seemed to suck out of the room, chilling 201's arms and neck.

A clunking sound echoed off the stone walls, and the dull whoosh of a fire springing to life. It sounded much like the boilers 201 had frequently heard near the Games Ring, the main source of heat for that region of Epsilon Circuit.

Before she could react, a roar exploded directly behind her, illuminating a row of tightly packed heads and shoulders, casting distorted shadows on the wall. She strained her neck, twisting sharply to witness fire flowing like water, billowing and creeping in clouds over the screaming figures behind her, blanketing its way towards 201.

201 froze, neck bent at an unnatural angle, mesmerized by the undulation of the flames, bright orange, red, with flecks of yellow, flowing, covering, consuming everything in its path. The wailing grew louder, figures flailing, arms pushing and struggling to break free, hair igniting and evaporating instantaneously. 201 cried out as she felt her flesh heat up, her hair inhaled by the flames, eyes and brains boiling within her skull. She crumpled to the ground, the stench of burning hair and flesh rising and settling on the sticky, blackened mess.

She was moving. 201 was revived by the scent of trees, earth and the coolness of the night air. Another, darker scent tainted the landscape, a cloying, sickening waft of something sour, like spilled cider and blood from the floor of the Games Circuit.

"Why do we have to do it this night?" asked an Officer, voice petulant.

"Because we lost the bet, so push that cart and we'll be finished and back drinking cider before you know it."

"Can't we just leave them here? What's the difference?"

"Because Pinnacle Officer Wilcox says they go in the pit. So they go in the pit. Now stop talking and keep pushing, only three more lots to go."

She felt herself tilt and fall, knocking against a layer of bones and charred flesh, the hollow sound reverberating in her consciousness.

Another load landed on top of her, crushing her further into the pit. Trapped in tightly filled blackness, she could see nothing more, the rhythmic sounds of bone clomping against bone filling the open air above.

21

That morning at line check, 201 looked to 232's usual place in the line of Internees, finding a gap in the procession. Squinting ahead, eyes swollen, she shuffled through with the rest of the Epsilon fellows, seating herself between two Internees that seemed vaguely familiar. They ignored her, rapidly demolishing their rations, making the odd comment or polite exchange about Fighter selection, training and the like.

201 contemplated her rations, hands shaking slightly as she gripped her utensil in one hand. A swift wave of unsteadiness hit her and she swayed, trying desperately to stay upright. The faces before her swam into her peripheral vision, warping and twisting. She looked to her left, watching the row of faces change from symmetrical to slanted, sagging, dough-like. Eyes fell from sockets, smiles grew impossibly wide, flesh eating away at the edges of mouths until only teeth and ragged flesh remained. Skin paled to yellow, waxen tones until they became grey, mottled, porous. Bodies, toned and muscular were stripped by tiny insects, uniforms dissolving into holes, shreds, until only strands were left hanging from bones, bleached white, piled one upon the other,

devoid of blood and flesh and life. The voices murmured around her, swirling and dancing, strange people talking of familiar things, forced enthusiasm and dull bravado resolutely in place to mask the truth. And it was that truth, that unbearable feeling of real, that made her say it aloud.

"You're all going to die."

277, shot her a look. 277 was a Fighter with light brown hair, handy with a zulfiqar, if 201 recalled correctly. "You say something, 201?"

201 smiled ruefully, eyes glazed over. She leaned in towards 277.

"You. Are. All. Going. To. Die." She smiled, leaning back on the ration bench, swinging her legs playfully. 277 gaped at her.

"Don't you feel it? Can't you see? You're all dead already. You just don't know it yet."

Tears prickled the edges of her eyes as she fixed her watery glare on 277. "And you're next. Your zulfiqar won't save you this time."

277 pushed her ration tray to the side, rising above 201, ready to strike. The other Internees backed off, clearing a space around them.

201 looked up at her, nodding acceptingly. She stood to her full height, opening her jumpsuit, peeling it down her shoulders. She stood, half covered, baring her chest to 277, arms outstretched.

"Do what you will. If you're dead already then I am dead along with you. Doesn't it feel good, to know you are now, at the end, unbroken after all?"

277 stepped back, turning to her fellow Epsilon Internees for support.

"Leave her, 277. She's clearly senseless."

201 laughed, a breathy, hoarse sound. "That is where you are wrong, 263. I have too much of my senses, too much sensation, there is just too much light..."

Officer Harold appeared at her side, hurriedly covering her with a robe. "Come 201, you are causing a fuss. You don't want to do this, they'll send you to Zeta."

"Officer Harold, you understand, don't you?" She looked at him imploringly as he clutched the fabric around her shoulders. "We're all dead. We're just waiting for the call."

A sharp jab in her side shocked her from her haze. The shot began to take effect, lurching her from alert to uncontrollably drowsy.

"Harold, why did you... what am I doing here?"

"Back to rations, all of you. 201 has just got herself a hold of some cider. It's clearly against regulations and she must be disciplined. Come now 201. Back to your chambers."

201 dragged her feet through the ration hall and back to her chamber, Harold taking most of her weight as she swayed, drowsy from the exertion.

"Why did you tell them that? I know I must not touch the cider in the Epsilon ring."

"Are you trying to get yourself thrown on the scrapheap? What did you think you were doing?"

"Just... telling everyone the truth. I'm dead, they're dead, what does it matter now? We're all just piles of bones in a pit. They crunch you know, when they break, it sounds like twigs and the dry leaves outside. Did you know, they make a hollow sound when they hit together, when they shift as another falls above. It's a hollow sound, but the sound of... something. It's like something I know, I've heard somewhere before, like a wooden log hollowed out by time. It's... beautiful."

Officer Harold stared at her, face pale with shock. "How did you..." He shuffled her through the door to her chamber. "You must not speak of this, any of this. Or... I do not know what your punishment will be. There will be no more talk, not like this, not ever again. Do you understand?"

201 swayed, a grin tickling the edges of her mouth.

"Do you understand!" he roared in her face, pushing her towards the bed. She fell gracelessly, a tangle of limbs, face squashed into the silk coverings. "So, go. Sleep now. Stay asleep for all I care. Just shut that big mouth, I'm warning you."

The door sucked shut, ruffling the hair over her eyes with a cool gust.

22

That night, 201 dreamed of a room, far grander than any chambers she had ever seen. The floor was made from wood, a large fire flickering in the far corner of the room. She found herself on a bed, dressed in what appeared to be a Beta jumpsuit. She could only see her legs and arms as she glanced around the room, catching the eye of what appeared to be a Resident Citizen, a Vendee. She knew his name was Yuri, however she could not ascertain anything else from his presence.

"Lie down." Yuri ordered. She felt herself recline on the bed, legs outstretched in what appeared to be a regulation seduction pose.

"I am displeased with the way you cleaned the floors today. There is still dirt in the corners."

"Forgive me, Resident Citizen Yuri." Her voice sounded strange to her ears, disembodied, lilting, somewhat higher in pitch than usual.

"Oh, I will forgive you, pretty one. But only after your penalty is served."

"But Resident Citizen Yuri, do you not desire me? Would you not rather take me instead?"

"No, I would not rather take you instead, perhaps later, if you demonstrate your willingness to my satisfaction. I would advise you not to speak again. I much prefer this." He shot out his fist, catching her in the jaw, the sharp pain aching almost instantly. He brought a leather belt, hidden in his other hand, down again and again on her back, stinging and burning through her white jumpsuit, which must be staining red by now.

Yuri laughed, a hollow, rasping sound. He brought the belt down again, laughing harder still.

201 awoke sheathed in sweat, shivering wildly, her face layered in tears. Her jaw ached and her back throbbed and stung, lasting through her hurried shower and lingering through the rest of the night as she tried, in desperation, to sleep.

23

The following days for 201 were fairly routine. Her muscle mass had dropped a little in the past month, sparing her the Games Ring for now. Reno had all but given up on nominating her as a Fighter, despite her clear talents for attacking and defensive maneuvers. She knew that she was far from the willowy, frail looking specimens in Beta and Omega Circuit. She was a long way from what she had endured before, body thin and pale, eyes wide and a sick, hollow feeling aching from her painfully concave stomach. But she was in Epsilon now. There were strength and agility requirements that she had not yet fulfilled, and testing was scheduled for this afternoon. She tried to put the thought out of her mind, preferring to bathe and prepare for her presentation in the regulation bathtub. She eyed her regulation grooming implements, the hours she was required to spend with combing, smoothing, brushing. She never used the comb, could not be bothered with the brush that made her scalp tickle and wasted time and effort she could have spent thinking, dreaming, exploring. Soothing music piped through to the bathroom, and 201 allowed her tension to drain away, to think of nothing and feel nothing.

24

That morning, after rations, 201 stepped tentatively into the chrome filled testing room, spotting only one Officer in attendance.

"Present, 201."

The door sucked shut behind her, causing her to flinch a little. 201 took a deep breath and stood tall, right foot forward slightly, chest curved slightly outwards and head tilted at what she hoped was a seductive angle.

"Wow. I mean... excellent." The Officer, Titan, was attractive, more so than the other Officers. In fact the majority of the Officers were balding, fat and generally repulsive in one way or another. 201 had never seen an Officer that looked anything remotely like Titan. She wondered where he had come from. His insignia read 24Y, unusually young for an Officer. He was tall, perhaps a little over six foot or so. His hair was a lightish blonde and stood out in all directions, a little longer than what passed for regulation length. His eyes were a striking blue-green and his features were pleasingly angular. But the main feature that attracted 201 was the kindness inherent in his face.

"Where did you come from?" she blurted.

"Pardon?"

201 cursed her quick mouth, hoping it would not get her in trouble this time. She searched his face for signs of annoyance and found none.

"Where did you come from?" she asked again, feeling bolder. "You don't look like the other Officers."

Titan laughed, a pleasing sound, the smile reaching his eyes. "No, I guess not. I'm from Ignatia schooling facility in Stenholme. I transferred for my first fellowship here. When we graduate, we have three fellowships, mainly to choose a suitable career for the future."

"Why would you want to come here? That doesn't make sense."

Titan paused. 201 lowered her head, shaking it. Too many questions, Harold always told her not to ask too many questions. She idly wondered what her punishment would be this time. Cleaning the fight ring was a particularly gruesome task, according to her fellow Internees. There was blood, and sometimes there was more than blood, more than she cared to think about.

"Sorry." She attempted a smile, it didn't seem to come off as she planned, earning a confused look from Titan.

"No, that's ok. I guess it is a strange choice. I wanted to help Internees and Vassals to improve themselves. My father thinks it's a ridiculous idea, pointless considering that Vassals are mostly single-use and replaced so often. I guess he doesn't really understand. He wants me to be a money lender, just like him, to follow in the tradition of my Grandfather's business, the way it was before the war."

"Huh."

"That's all? Huh?"

201 blanched, stepping away.

"No, I don't mean." Titan breathed out roughly. "I'm not going to punish you. I just thought it was interesting that you accepted what I said. All the Internees I have met tell me that Vassals are meant to serve, meant to be of service and obey, and maintain a physically pleasing appearance. They do not understand the concept of improving themselves, unless it is in a physical sense."

"But... you want to improve our minds."

Titan's eyes widened. "Yes! You understand! You are the first one to understand! This is fantastic!" He clasped his hands together and began to pace.

201's hair began to bristle. A cold, creeping feeling started to rise in the back of her neck. She shivered slightly, hand reaching out to smooth down the hairs on her forearm.

"Titan. I don't know who you have spoken to about this, but I suggest you keep it to yourself." Her voice sounded far away, almost as if someone else was speaking for her.

Titan looked at her as if she had lost her mind. He tilted his head to the side, holding her gaze.

"But why? I have always postulated in my theories that Internees and Vassals can think for themselves, can create, make decisions, even lead..."

"Titan!" 201's loud voice echoed in the silence that followed. Titan looked confused, waiting for 201 to continue.

"I would not claim to be an authority on what goes on here at FERTS. I don't know why I feel this, why I'm telling you this. But I must say this to you. What you are doing is dangerous. You must not discuss this with anyone, especially not here."

"But why?"

"Because it's true. All of what you say in your theories. It's true."

Titan slid to the ground, settling himself in a cross-legged position. 201 lowered herself to the ground to join him, mimicking his pose.

"I knew it," Titan muttered. "I knew it was true... hoped it was. Now I hear you speaking and I know it to be true, even it you had not told me you believed me, you are exactly what I have been waiting for."

"No, you don't understand. This is not all there is. Your theories are true, everything you say is true. The part you do not understand is that they already know. They already know about this, about us, about everything."

"Who?"

"The Officers, the higher rankers, even some of the lower ranks, even some of the Vendees. They know. I tell you this is dangerous because they know, they just don't care."

Titan looked horrified, then disgusted. "How can you know... That can't be. Someone would have said something, done something."

"Who would speak? Who would disagree? The Officers? Their very existence depends on the Internees and Vassals being trained to serve. Or maybe the Vendees, the Resident Citizens? They have a Vassal to fulfil their every fantasy, their domestic duties. The Vassals provide Sires, all their needs are satisfied. Why would anyone speak out?"

"I still don't understand. How do you know this?"

201 was silent for a moment. "I wish I knew the answer to that question." She absently scratched behind her ear. "It's as if I did not know until you started to ask me those questions. But it is also as if the answers have been there all the time."

Titan stared at her, shaking his head in astonishment.

"It can't be true. It can't be. Intuition. You have it. You actually have it. Intuition," he muttered excitedly, almost to himself, repeating the word once more under his breath.

"What is that?"

Titan's eyes gleamed as he gestured excitedly.

"You don't know? Of course, what am I thinking? I have read about this, I never dreamed I could possibly meet anyone with this real, tangible ability. As far as I know, no Resident Citizen has ever shown signs of intuition, but I have heard stories, back from times before the war, when the likes of Internees and Vassals, though they weren't called that back then, lived very long lives, had knowledge of the times before, knowledge of times in present, and knowledge of futures yet to come."

"They weren't called... so what were the Internees and Vassals called back then?"

Titan looked up at her, tilting his head to the side with a slight smile tugging at his lips.

"Women."

25

201 went to bed excited, mind swimming with all the things she and Titan had discussed. She was most excited about what she had discovered, what she had known without being told.

How long have I been like this?

Are there others like me?

The piped music in her bedroom changed, slowing to a lethargic pace. Every night it had made her fall asleep almost instantly, the waves of soothing melody cocooning her in a kind of artificial warmth and contentment. As she drifted, voices weaved through her head.

"It alters the Internee's state of alertness. Just a simple process really, the regular pulse induces brain waves conducive to sleep. Switches their vitals to sleep mode, if you will. Added effects are slowed respiration, promotion of somnolence, that sort of thing..."

"Hello?" 201 sat upright, wildly looking around the room for signs of who had just spoken.

No answer came. 201's mind raced, voices and thoughts layering upon each other until she could no longer understand the chatter. 201 did not fall to sleep for the rest of the night.

26

The next morning her results printed through the slot near her bedside table.

Strength: fair

Agility: poor

Muscle mass: fair

She rubbed at her eyes, the desire for sleep overwhelming her senses, trying vainly to understand the words before her. It was only now, with the morning light filtering through her chamber that she realized that Titan had not tested her, not once.

She scowled at the results, insulted. Why would Titan assume she was not strong, not agile enough to fight? She had lost some muscle mass, it was true, but she was fiercely quick and her strength belied her small frame. She supposed her muscle mass would be somewhere around 26 by now, much closer to Vassal regulation.

Perhaps Titan had a good reason to write her results in this way. She recalled Harold's words to her.

Once you are scarred, you cannot return to Omega.

A scar would narrow her options even further. She would have no choice but to be forced to fight in Epsilon, put to work in Kappa, or, and this would be worst, relegated to Zeta Circuit. Nobody returned from Zeta Circuit, this was common knowledge. Perhaps Titan was trying to assist her in some way, though she could not understand why an Officer would behave in this manner. She had no desire to be a Vassal, but perhaps that was the only way out, the only way to get free of FERTS, at least for a time.

Scanning the results, she spotted a recommendation scrawled near the bottom of the page.

If muscle mass continues to fall, recommend transfer to Omega Circuit for Vassal training.

27

201 continued her efforts to reduce her muscle mass. At ration times, she ate only half of her regulation protein. She felt her strength reducing day by day, and each night, she compensated by going through some random stretches she had learned from Reno's training sessions. She had taken to plugging the piped music with a towel during her nightly training to avoid distractions. She jogged on the spot and settled in to perform some deep stretches, testing her flexibility with each push. Somehow she knew, somehow she just knew why they wanted the Internees to be thin, delicate.

They are easier to control that way.

She gripped the stone beneath her, balancing on the balls of her feet, edging her body towards the floor in a slow, downward motion.

They are easier to control...

The voice came from deep within her. She could not ascertain the origin, but she knew these words to be true.

Officer Reno's voice filtered through her mind, the press of his finger marking her forehead.

You have this. Use it.

So to the Officers she would appear thin, delicate, fragile, even. But she would only appear so in a superficial capacity. Beneath the surface she would be strong, stronger than any of them might imagine. She would be lithe, sharp, and most importantly, she would be swift.

28

"Line check!"

201 shuffled out with all the other Epsilon Internees as the roll was called, each Internee replying in turn. The suction lock to her chamber unlocked with a rush of cool air. She stood, dressed in her regulation red jumpsuit, aligning side by side with her doormates. The Officer stood above the railing, looking down on the walkways filled with Epsilon fellows. His face was dark, impassioned, his uniform neatly pressed and shoes brightly shined.

The Officer read out the FERTS Requital, 201 mouthing the words as the other Internees answered the call with an enthusiastic response.

"The following are to present to the testing rooms. 207, 275, 201, 254 and 255. The rest are to present for training after the scheduled ration room visit."

Fantastic, 201 mused. She briefly panicked, wondering if her efforts to lose muscle mass had been enough. She had eaten far less than standard ration for so long, even though her stomach cried out to be filled. She had also banned herself from the gym. Instead she had taken to actually using the unpleasant face creams, brushes and hair ointments and had even forced herself to practice the tedious eyelash flutters and coy looks in her evaluation mirror.

She followed the hall to the testing room, finding the waiting area empty. She wondered briefly if she had followed the wrong marker but the precise testing room lettering, bright in burnished metal, stared back at her.

The testing room was empty save for a large, broad shouldered Officer. 201 stiffened, feeling a coldness envelop her shoulders and ruffle the hairs on her forearms. Something was not right.

The door sucked shut behind her.

The Officer's name was Morton, and his face was huge, with a pronounced jaw and a dark scowl ruffling his bushy brows. He held a clipboard that seemed pitifully small compared to his frame.

"Strip."

"What?"

"Strip."

"That's not what the testers do! You're supposed to test for muscle mass and…"

201 felt the blow throb against her cheek after she hit the ground. The pain started quietly, growing to an unbearable intensity as she gritted her teeth against the wail that escaped her throat.

"Don't talk again. I think we understand each other now."

201 drew in a deep breath, stood to her full height and looked him directly in the eye. He would not see her cry. That would be for later, and would be only for her.

Morton looked back, bored. He gestured at her clothes. "Strip. I won't ask again."

201 slid off the jumpsuit, standing upright yet again.

"You're not very good at this, are you?"

201 stared back, eyes intensely focused on the space between his brows.

Morton pushed her to the ground and undid his trousers. 201 turned her head to the side, preferring not to see the repulsiveness of the Officer's body up close. He tried to push inside her, even though her body closed up, refusing to let him in. After much swearing and pushing he forced himself inside, tearing her from within as she felt heat and a horrible stinging, and the trickle of blood down her thighs. The pain grew with each moment, jarring her insides as she clenched her fists at her sides. 201 squeezed her eyes tightly against the image of Morton's beard, sticky with saliva, as he panted into her face.

29

201 did not remember how she got back to her room. She awoke to find her sheets damp with sweat and her face sticking to her pillow. She slid carefully across the covers and edged her way to the bathroom, trying to ignore the stabbing pain inside her body as she moved her legs deliberately, one after the other. The light in the bathroom was too bright and hurt her eyes. She took two more steps into the bathroom before emptying her stomach into the toilet bowl.

Turning on the shower she stepped inside, the water scaldingly hot until she adjusted the flow. She cleansed and bathed in regulation order to remove the stink of Morton on her body. First soap, then the regulation facial cleanser, the pungent smelling shampoo, a second application of shampoo, then conditioner. Another wash with the soap, lathering it up until it bubbled all over her hands, washing each part, each section in turn until everything squeaked with cleanliness. She staggered out of the shower to fetch her robe. She sat at the evaluation mirror, first combing, then smoothing her hair with fragrant oils. Then came the drying and shaping, and lastly, the brushing. She followed regulation step by step, using the skin creams, the eyelash oil, lip softener and body lotions. She trimmed her toenails and fingernails, and set about whitening the insides of her nails with the special crayon that she had never used before this day. Sitting at the evaluation mirror, she nodded, seated primly, dressed in her robe, hands shaking slightly, hair perfectly coiffed, skin smooth and each part of her body perfectly manicured. The moon filtered through her sliver of a window into the semi-darkness of her room as her reflection stared defiantly back.

30

That night 201 was restless, images of Morton and his flushed, sweaty face swam before her eyes. Without her consent, more images came, scattering, flickering, rising and falling. First it was a flash here or there of another room, another uniform pressed against her small frame. The pictures in her mind rose up, beginning slowly, gaining momentum until everything was moving forward in rapid motion. Before long the memories flooded her mind, overtaking her, breaking open the walls she had so carefully built around the room that she did not dare enter, the room from which she had hidden the key and obscured the lock for all time.

His insignia read Officer Jorg. The 42Y next to his identification seared into her eyes, opening gateways to a time, a world she swore she would never revisit.

"Shh. Don't you dare make a sound. Someone will hear and then you will be punished."

He leaned closer, his thinning blonde hair tickling her throat.

"And you know what the punishment will be, don't you, little one?"

She squirmed, attempting to break free of his hold.

"They will send you to Zeta Circuit. That is where the ones like you will go if you do not keep quiet." His fingers slid underneath her uniform, searching, making her squirm in discomfort.

"You are far too tense, this won't do. I guess will have to use your mouth instead. Open up for me now, if you don't I will make you will wish you had." She shook her head, mouth clamped shut. He gripped her jaw, squeezing hard. His eyes, blank and lifeless fixed upon hers. "Do not make me say it again."

She complied, trying to keep her eyes trained on anything other than what he was doing. She gagged, her airway choked, tears escaping the corners of her eyes. She steadied her gaze on the window, the thin sliver of light coming through, the sounds of the forest outside. She closed her eyes and imagined herself somewhere else, somewhere green and wooded, somewhere that was not surrounded by polished metal and marble that clacked under her feet. Her mind seemed to split in two, right at that moment. She was running, running not from something but towards something, she did not know what that something would be, but she knew it was better, better than this, better than the choking feeling in her throat, the obscene moans coming from above her head.

He threw her back then, down to the floor, zipping up his uniform pants as he left. She sat on the floor, head bowed, tears running down her cheeks and diverting into her ears, filling them, making them uncomfortably warm. She gasped for breath, *blinking down at her insignia, the 12Y glowing smugly back at her.*

201 did not make it to the bathroom this time. She heaved, crouched over on one knee, spilling mostly water and what looked like blood onto the polished floor. She was motionless, watching the pool of dark liquid soak over the striations, edging further and further from her body as she did nothing to soak up the flow.

I was just a little one! So small, how could I not remember?

I thought it happened to someone else. A story I had heard, just a nightmare, a horrible dream I had one night.

How could I not remember?

She heaved again, making no effort this time to protect her robe. The cold from the stone floor seeped into her body but yet she stayed, hunched over, body shuddering as she gasped for air. She sank further into the stone, curling in on herself. A sound was coming from somewhere, a low whine, breaking into a howl, and tapering off into whispering sobs. It was only when she paused to swallow a breath that she realized that the sound was coming from deep within her. The tears warmed her face, rushing down in rivulets, streaking her neck, seeping in to the hollow of her collarbone. The breeze from the window cooled the mess on her robe, clinging cruelly to her chilled skin, and still she stayed. The bed beckoned to her, snug and crisp, and yet she stayed.

31

The next morning hit 201 with a wave of nausea. She peeled herself off the stone floor, cold and sticky, barely making it to the bathroom before throwing up what little contents her stomach had left. Leaning on the bowl, face sticky with tears, she wheezed repeatedly, trying to catch her breath. A faint sound hummed from the bedroom, the printer spitting out the results from yesterdays 'test'. She held back another urge to throw up, bracing herself on the bowl and lifting herself to a standing position. She looked straight at the mirror, chin jutted out in defiance. She looked no different, save for her reddened eyes and tear streaked face. Perhaps she should look different, but then again it had not happened the first time, why would it happen now? She felt sure the others would know, just by looking at her, what Morton had done.

She pooled towels on the floor, mopping up the dried liquid, peeled the crusted robe from her body and threw the whole filthy pile into the washing slot. She showered for longer than usual this time, making sure to clean herself thoroughly and methodically, attempting to scrub away any reminders of Morton from her body. It didn't work, but she dressed and groomed according to regulation and sat back against the bed, ripping the results from the slot.

Promotion to Omega successful. Transfer completion underway.

201 could not smile.

32

Wilcox stretched lazily from his plush, velvet draped bed. On his left side was a Vassal, Beth 23 something. He couldn't remember and he supposed it didn't really matter. What mattered was she was an 18Y, blonde and had long, lean legs and wide blue eyes. He looked over at her face, scrunched up in sleep. She stirred, snuffling and scratching at her eye. When she focused her gaze, she found herself staring up into his impassive face. Her face was unsure, searching, slowly forming into a practised, seductive pout. What she did not understand was that Wilcox was done with her.

"Out." Confusion crossed her features before settling into a dutiful smile, head bowed.

"Are you deaf? I said out." He kicked at her shin, pushing her to the edge of the bed. She scurried to the floor next to the bed, stopping only to pick up her jumpsuit on the way out the door.

Wilcox laid back, frowning. If only there was a way to make the Beths more dutiful, more obedient. He would look into that, perhaps study the current batch, find another way to shape their nature, make them more receptive. There was always something to improve, always something to adjust. The Beths had been troublesome in the past, but over time, they had become something closer to the ideal. He would know the time when he had achieved greatness, but that moment had not arrived just yet. Now was a time for planning, for development, and for further research. The Resident Citizens had become more receptive to his methods in recent years, but again, this had taken more time than expected. Since the dark times, there had been years of flux and chaos, society had become warlike, tribal. There was no order, no hierarchy, no understanding of status or proper place.

The wars had been gradual, building up in many parts of the land until war became all encompassing. Technology had become masterful for these crude purposes, and weapons had become progressively more effective, wiping out thousands instead of hundreds in mere seconds. The technology was not limited to one side, however, and vast numbers were decimated simultaneously. As troop numbers had dwindled, slain in combat or lost to defection, the forces gradually began to lose their hold on conquered territories. The remaining troops, weary of battle, began to overthrow the elected governments until the lands were plunged into lawlessness. Resources dwindled and the remaining inhabitants fled to the relative safety of the more isolated territories.

Before long, the society Wilcox had previously known had all but shut down. The relative stability of government, rule of law, medical and emergency services, each dissolved shortly after the collapse of government. Some valiantly attempted to continue their assistance to the community, only to be ransacked by marauders. Many fled to save their own lives. A few had elected to stay, only to be slain for their efforts. The order of society had been flayed open. Soon, the desire to take and destroy were unfettered, the vigilantes fighting amongst each other for the few meagre resources left untouched.

After a time, the territories began to regroup. The hordes, never content to stay in one place, had departed in search of fresh conquests. Communities were fractured, broken. Many attempted to build, to gather some kind of order into the townships, but most were aimless, unsure of where to begin.

Wilcox had been the only one who had seen the real cause of society's ills. Wilcox could see to the heart of matters, that is what people had come to expect of him. He was undisputed and unchallenged as the wisest in the township of Evergreen. In times of chaos, the people from surrounding townships had come to him repeatedly with their various problems, their petty disputes, their conflicts. Men fought over women, custody of children, the acquisition of property and livelihood, and generally complained about the complications of life in the townships. All this time, Wilcox had seen, had heard, and understood. Wilcox possessed that which the others did not. A pure, clear ideal, the vital spark to begin again, reborn in a new image. The cause of all these disputes, all these clashes, the very dissonance at the heart of the people of Evergreen, of social structure, of society as a whole, was simple, so simple, in fact, that it was staring them right in the face the whole time.

Women.

33

Wilcox had been a young man then, a scientist during the old times, he had run the most prestigious of facilities in medical testing and genetic study. Although he had thought of himself as a visionary in progressing in the field of medical testing and analysis, the truth was that he was essentially a glorified prison guard. He ran a number of facilities for a private company, contracted by the military in times of war. The complex housed the usual, prisoners of war, enemies of the government, refugees without proper identification and the like. He spent his days testing, probing, studying. He wanted to know the inner workings of the human body, the very mechanisms from which life is created. He performed dissections, hundreds of them. Towards the end, when society had begun to collapse, he knew he did not have much time. He began dissections on random subjects, studying those with certain characteristics, discarding the ones that did not meet his standards. He would find a way to engineer the human form, to shape it, to hone and refine. In the end the prisoners were liquidated on Wilcox's order, discarded in pits deep in the forest. The only safe areas that remained were isolated farmlands and sleepy valleys, far from the major cities and industrial regions. Wilcox fled, along with his fellow scientists and settled in a remote township far from the conflicts.

Life went on, though it was unrecognizable from Wilcox's perspective. There was too much fighting, quarrelling, and a general disorder about the place that Wilcox found distasteful. The townspeople came to him for advice, as he was clearly well educated and knowledgeable about the ordered way in which to run a trouble-free society. During the wars, many of the brightest and most celebrated members of society were lost in the ensuing battles. Wilcox was unique in this way. Not only had he survived, but he had an opportunity in his new township, a new beginning in which to start his work.

The planning was the most frustrating part. He knew that for what he had planned, no matter how deficient the inhabitants were in terms of education, it was clear that something dramatic needed to happen. Fear, the great motivator, would this time become his trusted companion. The townspeople were weary, tired of wars, tired of quarrels. Wilcox would show them a new way, a safer way, a more ordered way for society to progress.

He set about in contacting some of his old colleagues from his days in the military detention industry. Many of the former guards and soldiers had become mercenaries after the war, content to move from township to township, taking what they needed, food, supplies and women. Wilcox decided on a deal based on mutual understanding of needs. The mercenaries would play their part, and for their reward they would be allowed their choice of women in the town, as many resources as they could carry, and plentiful food and drink. In return, Wilcox would ask for nothing, save for their perpetual silence. It seemed an odd exchange at the time, though the mercenaries weren't overly concerned with asking questions. They would gain what they needed, and they would be on their way.

34

The township of Evergreen awakened as normal that morning, food was becoming more plentiful as the townspeople went about planting and harvesting crops, both in their own land, and in communal growing spaces. Metalwork had begun in earnest, the mass-produced technology of times before had faded, requiring a relearning of making things by hand. There were some animals, though they had been sparse at first. A careful breeding program had ensured that the township was provided with milk and later, hand made cheeses and cream. Baking was done by hand, using fire and clay ovens. Flour was hand ground by stones and clothing was made using bone needle and twine, or wool when it became available. Cider was brewed from apples, as grains were as yet in short supply. Children played in the townships, making games out of sticks, leaves and pebbles. One of these children, Gerda, was the first to see them.

She was playing near a brook at the far end of the town, her leaf floating down the stream as she ran, hair bouncing, poking her stick out every now and then to push the leaf when it got caught in the tightly gathered twigs that lined the edge. She hummed a tune, something that she had not heard before, just a spontaneous, aimless melody, her voice rising and falling with the rushing of the water.

Gerda heard the hoofbeats long before she saw them. Raising her hand to the sky, she shielded her face from the sun, squinting towards the mountains that surrounded the township of Evergreen. Dust and drift seeds glowed in the light, rising up from the ground and gently wafting past the shade of her arm. Then she saw them. Three shapes, rounded dark shapes in the distance, gradually becoming more formed as they emerged from the haze. But it was not three but five, no, ten, so many, so many of them, the hoofbeats drowning out the running of the water, her stick dropped to the ground, leaf forgotten, she screamed.

35

The people of Evergreen huddled in the town's main hall, shivering in the cold as the rain fell steadily outside. A fire was built in the oversized hearth, flames burning bright, as yet too new to be producing much heat. The townspeople was mostly comprised of men, the majority of the women taken by the men who had ridden through town, stealing and destroying everything they touched.

"Friends, this will not do. This cannot go on."

Nobody had observed Wilcox's ascent to the lectern, an old wooden teacher's stand salvaged from an abandoned school nearby.

"You see what they have done to us, what we have become?" He stared resolutely into the crowd, meeting each eye in turn. "We are afraid, always afraid of what is to come. This is no way for our township to progress forward. The men who... came here today." He looked around sympathetically, a sombre grimace crossing his features. "They will continue to come until there is nothing left for us to rebuild. And do you know why they will always return, citizens?" The gathering was silent, awaiting his next words with wide eyes. "Women. They come for the women and they will continue to come, destroying all we have built, everything we own!" He paused for breath, lowering his voice. "So, friends, citizens." He smiled an encouraging smile, eyes dancing with something that could have been tears, or perhaps joy. "We must remove the enticement." He slapped the lectern in time with his words. "Take away the prize and these mercenaries will have no reason to come to Evergreen. The remaining men will be free to defend the township, and the women will be safe from the hands of these interlopers!" A light applause smattered through the hall, most too shocked from the days events to respond.

"Think! This could be the start, a new beginning and a new way of living. There will be no more confusion, no more conflict, we can grow the township, make something with what we have been given!" The group clapped, more enthusiastically this time. "It may not seem so, given the events of today, but this could be the most important day in the history of this township! Today was the day we began to protect what is rightfully ours!" A hesitant clapping rang out.

"The women of Evergreen will be safe!" More applause.

"Our beloved Evergreen will be protected. There will be no more trouble from the interlopers!" The applause grew, filling the hall and roaring in his ears. "The time for action is upon us!"

"This is the day the true township of Evergreen begins. To set an example, a precedent from there was none. We will rebuild in a new image. A model of stability! Of order! A society of which we can be proud to call our own. We will build a new beginning!" A great cheer erupted, echoing though the halls, rising with Wilcox's hands as they raised to the roof of the hall, stretching up towards the sky.

36

Three weeks later, before dawn, Wilcox had gathered together an additional group of mercenaries in the small south western township of Riversberg. In the still darkness they stole through the town, removing the few women left behind in the raid. They did not bother to announce their presence, just entered each room, placing a warning hand over each woman's mouth, loading each of them into the transport wagon. They were stealthy, and many of the townspeople remained asleep during the visitations. As they moved from house to house, many were still unaware that anything was amiss. However one girl, unable to sleep, had witnessed the raids on the houses, her tunic barely covering to her knees since she had grown so much this past year. She was ten, her parents had been lost in the war and she had stayed in the care of Wesley, an ex-soldier and defector who wanted nothing more to do with further conflicts. The girl was no fool, and seeing the mercenaries taking the women and girls from their homes, she rushed to her room, gathering up as many clothes as she could find to fill her satchel. She made sure to pack her knife, the blankets from her bed and the warmest clothes she could find. She grabbed her kit that Wes had given her for her tenth birthday, containing flint, an army issue pocket knife, a miniature first aid kit, a tiny compass and a ball of twine. She loaded the bag with a small pot, a fork, spoon, and a bag of potatoes from the kitchen before running breathlessly into Wesley's room.

"Wes?"

"Mmph? What is it Raf?" He covered one eye, blinking sleepily.

"I have to go. There are mercenaries outside. They are taking all the women and girls. They'll take me if I stay."

Wesley bolted upright, rushing to peer through the window to see the wagon, its wooden cage crawling with grasping hands and feet. He felt a tug to his sleeve and crouched down to face Rafaella.

"I have to go, Wes. I don't have much time." Wesley looked around in desperation, stilling as understanding crossed his features.

"You're a brave girl, Raf. I would come with you if I thought it would not arouse suspicion. I will tell them you were taken during the raids of two weeks past. You must find somewhere far away and you must not send word to me, it's not safe." He rummaged next to the bed and pulled out a small Amidal pistol.

"Take this."

"What about you?"

"Ssh. I've got the old Harron. It fits my hands but it's much too big for you to shoot. Come on now." He ushered her through to the back door.

Once in the doorway they did not risk words for fear of discovery. Wesley placed his hand on Rafaella's shoulder, eyes bright with tears, his salt and pepper beard glinting in the moonlight. Rafaella hugged him fiercely, forcing herself not to cry. She took one last look at his face and turned to face the field behind the house. She ran softly, quietly, avoiding branches and anything that might make a sound. She ran towards water, just as Wesley had taught her back when she was very young. The Elan river was large, and stretched for many miles to the north-east of Riversberg. The rushing of the water would cover the sound of her boots as she ran, and the water would keep her from becoming thirsty on her journey. She concentrated on nothing but her footing, the sound of the water, the animals in the field, the rhythm of her breathing. She kept her eyes soft, allowing herself to focus on the immediate periphery for any movement that was out of the ordinary. She kept her pace brisk but steady, making sure not to expend too much energy all in one go. Before long a fuzzy blue haze surrounded her, signaling the dawn's arrival. The need to find cover became apparent, before sunrise could expose her movements in the open field. She turned to her right, heading towards something resembling an old school. She would never have stopped for a barn or a toolshed, too much chance of being discovered during the course of the day. There were no longer any active schools in Riversberg, and an abandoned school most likely would not be disturbed for any reason she could sensibly imagine. She rushed inside, just as the first glimpses of dawn peeked over the field, illuminating the tips of the grass.

Exhausted, her adrenaline caught up with her at once. Now indoors in relative safety, standing still for the first time, she felt her body beginning to shut down. Her heart was racing but she could feel the sleepiness creeping in as the rush subsided. The school was tiny, with a low roof made for people much shorter than most of the townspeople of Riversberg, rows of dark wooden desks lined up before a small hand carved bench at the head of the room. She doubted this school had been used for many years. It looked nothing like the pre-war schools Wes had described, with their clean white walls and arched windows. A few books lay in a shelf in the corner of the room, caked with dust and cobwebs. Rafaella pulled out her flask, taking a long drink and settled herself with a warm blanket behind the podium, using her satchel as a pillow. This would do for now, she would sleep, regain her strength, and resume her journey after nightfall.

37

That night Rafaella continued her path along the Elan river, stopping periodically to refill her flask from the running water below. She shifted the satchel from shoulder to shoulder, cursing her decision to pack potatoes of all things.

Why didn't I bring corn? I could have packed many more and they don't weigh nearly as much.

She did not know how many hours she had trekked along the river in a north-easterly direction, she was only aware of the pain in her feet, and how her legs ached with each passing step. She slumped to rest on a rock for a moment to take a rest and catch her breath. It was only then that she heard it.

Someone was crying. It sounded to Rafaella's ears to be nearby, a quiet, breathy sob. Rafaella tensed, reaching for the gun. She had learned to shoot at a young age, and since most people were likely to be comparatively taller and stronger, it was the best defence she had. Another cry started up, thin and soft, the shaky sound barely reaching her ears.

Rafaella took a deep breath, hoisting herself from the relative comfort of her rock. She crept towards the sound, careful not to alert anyone to her presence just in case it was a trap. She settled herself behind a small shrub by the river and peered out at the small clearing.

The girl was young, younger than Rafaella herself, perhaps seven or so, it was hard to tell in this light. She perched on a rock, dressed only in a thin tunic and cloth trousers. Her face, illuminated by the moonlight, was wet with tears. Her hands covered most of her face while also obscuring Rafaella's approach. Rafaella edged silently around the shrub, softly keeping to the shadows surrounding the clearing until she appeared at the side of the rock, just to the girl's left. She crouched down, trying to make herself look as unthreatening as possible.

"Hey."

The girl looked up at Rafaella, eyes widened in shock and fear as she scrabbled away, tumbling off her rock and crunching into a pile of leaves.

"No, wait. It's okay. I'm not one of them. You're safe here."

The girl raised her head, a shock of black curls falling into her face. She wiped her eyes, sniffling, pushing her hair out of her eyes, only to have it fall back down again.

"Who... Who are you?"

"I'm Rafaella. I escaped from the township of Riversberg when the mercenaries took all the other girls from my town. What's your name?"

"Cal.. Caltha."

"Pleased to meet you, Caltha." She reached out her hand.

Caltha straightened, remembering her manners.

"Pleased to meet you too." Caltha took Rafaella's hand, trying to steady herself and attempted a shaky smile.

"It's okay. I'm scared too."

Caltha scowled, crossing her arms in front of her.

"I'm not scared."

Rafaella chuckled to herself and put a hand on Caltha's shoulder.

"That's good. I'm glad you're not. It's just... It's okay if you do get scared. So don't worry too much okay?"

"Okay." Caltha shivered. They regarded each other for a moment, unsure of what to say next.

Caltha shivered again, drying her tears with irritated swipes of her palm. Rafaella rummaged in her satchel, pulling out her warmest tunic.

"Uh... Here, put this on. It'll keep you warm."

Caltha edged tentatively over and shrugged into the tunic. It hung like a dress over her knees, almost reaching her ankles.

"It is warm." She breathed a shaky breath, rubbing the wool at her elbow.

"How old are you?"

"I'm six. My birthday is the 5th of January," she announced proudly.

"Oh. Well I'm ten. Uh... My birthday is the 28th of October."

"You're a lot bigger than me." Caltha regarded her curiously, eyes scanning upward.

Rafaella smiled. "Don't worry, I'm sure you'll get bigger too. You've got some growing to do."

"Yeah, but my Ma is small. I think I'm gonna be short."

"Well if you're short, you can kick people in the shins."

Caltha giggled, a warm, bubbly sound. She paused after a moment, face going solemn.

"What happened to your Ma?" Rafaella moved closer to Caltha, settling herself on the rock.

"The men took her. She told me to run away before they came through the door, so I did. I didn't even get time to take any food with me."

"Well, I've got an idea. Why don't we team up? I've got some warm clothes and a little bit of food. I'm sure if we join forces we can do better than on our own. I'm good at finding things, and fighting, I'm not big enough to take on any grown ups yet but I'm pretty good, I guess."

Caltha was thoughtful for a moment before a wide grin broke across her face.

"I'll team up with you! Um... I'm good at some things. Like... um..."

Rafaella looked on, encouragingly.

"I can cook," she mumbled.

"Well that's good. Because I can't, and I've got a couple of potatoes that need cooking. I've only got a little pot that Wes used to boil tea on the fire."

"Wow. You've got potatoes? Oh wow! I'll wash them in the river. You get the firewood. Oh... wait. How can you start a fire now? It's night time and my glass won't work because there's no sun."

Rafaella smiled to herself, the kid was smart. That was a good sign if they were going to team up. She really didn't want to get stuck with someone who didn't know what they were doing, especially in this kind of unknown, hostile terrain.

"Don't worry, I'll take care of it."

Rafaella busied herself collecting kindling while Caltha washed the dirt off the potatoes and cut them into quarters, placing them into the pot with some water from the stream. Rafaella hunted around the base of each tree, picking up the driest twigs and sticks. There would be no logs tonight, she carried no axe and logs needed days to dry out, there just wasn't time to waste on such pursuits. She stayed close to the clearing, making sure she could see the moon's direction at all times. She picked out some dry moss, and selected the thickest branches that had fallen to the ground. Rafaella gathered rocks and laid them in a tight circle to create a barrier. She then laid the moss down in the kindling, took out her knife and scratched the flint on to the moss until sparks began to fly. The moss began to glow and smoke, sparks joining together to form a line until it ignited, lighting up the kindling and catching on the larger sticks. She blew gently at the base of the small fire, careful not to blow out the flames. After a time the fire began to sustain itself, radiating a dry warmth, not yet enough to produce a steady heat. She sat back on her heels to find Caltha watching her, mouth open in wonder.

"How'd you do that? That was amazing!"

"Wes used to use flint to make fires when he was in the army. It's a lot easier than rubbing sticks together. He said as long as you've got a spark you can build a fire anywhere." She smiled to herself, thinking of Wesley and wondering what he was doing right at this moment.

"Who's Wes?"

"He looked after me, I lived with him. He taught me a lot of stuff he learned when he was in combat. I guess we're lucky he did, or we wouldn't be eating tonight."

"He sounds pretty clever. So, do I put the pot on now?"

"No. Not yet, we need to get some coals going before we can do that. Why don't you help me get some more sticks while we're waiting?"

Caltha followed Rafaella around the edges of the clearing, picking up twigs as she went and handing them to Rafaella, who promptly threw most of them away.

Caltha finally stopped, hands on hips. Rafaella sensed the lack of movement and turned to investigate the reason why Caltha was no longer following her carefully selected path.

"Why are you throwing my sticks away? Don't you like them?"

"They're green. That means they're not dried out yet. Which also means they won't burn."

"Oh." Caltha stopped, unsure of what to do next. "So how do you know if they're green? They don't look green. They look the same as the ones you've got in your hand."

Rafaella carefully placed her bundle of sticks on the ground and crouched next to Caltha. "See this one?" She held it up for Caltha to inspect.

"Yeah, it doesn't look any different. How am I supposed to know?"

"Watch this."

Rafaella gripped the twig in both hands and pulled. The twig bent in the middle, flexing and twisting in her grasp. She then picked a stick from her own pile and repeated the movement, causing the stick to snap in two. Caltha's face lit up with a grin, looking from one stick to the other.

"So all you have to do, if you're not sure whether a twig is green..."

"Is to snap it!" Caltha clapped her hands.

"Exactly." Rafaella gathered up her sticks and wandered, circling the remaining trees for any loose twigs she might have missed. She smiled to herself as she heard the sounds of enthusiastic snapping and cracking following behind her.

When they returned to the fire, Rafaella hung the pot from a branch perched between two forked sticks driven in to the ground. Before long, the water began to bubble as the two settled in beside the fire to warm their hands.

When the potatoes were ready, Rafaella grabbed a heavy tunic to hold the pot and drained it out near the water's edge. When she returned Caltha decided the best option was to mash the lot and they ate from the pot, sharing a spoon. When they were finished they rinsed the pot in the stream and Rafaella laid out her blankets near the fire. Caltha looked on anxiously.

"What is it?"

"I didn't bring any blankets. Or pillows or anything."

Rafaella sighed, patting the blanket underneath her.

"Come on. I can't let you freeze." Caltha bounded over and climbed under the covers, elbowing Rafaella in the process.

"Ow! Watch those, you could cut someone with them!"

"Sorry," Caltha said distractedly, too excited by the thought of a warm bed and a fire for the night. Rafaella arranged the satchel so it lay crosswise, barely big enough for both to use as a pillow.

As they lay there listening to the crinkle and snap of the fire, Caltha turned from her side to lay flat to face the stars.

"Rafaella?"

"Hm?"

"Before you came along I hadn't eaten for three days. I had to walk around all night so I could keep warm. I'm glad I met you."

"Yeah, me too." Rafaella smiled into the satchel, nestling down for sleep.

"Um... Rafaella?"

"Yeah?"

"I can't sleep. Can you tell me a story?"

"I don't know. I know some, but they come from books. I don't really remember how they go."

"Can you make one up? Just until I go to sleep?"

"Um... okay. Uh... Long ago, in a township far away, there were two sisters called... Hett and... Wenda. Hett was the eldest, and she looked after Wenda wherever they went. One day... they set off on an adventure, an adventure that would change their lives forever..." Rafaella went on, trying to find the right words to keep the story going. After a short while she heard the soft sounds of Caltha's snores rising up into the air. Rafaella shuffled down, burying her head in her satchel, thankful for the warmth of the blankets, Caltha's sleeping form and the glowing embers of the fire. It was just as well Caltha had fallen asleep, she had no idea where the story was going anyway.

38

Many weeks passed and Caltha and Rafaella had become increasingly convinced that they would not find anywhere to call home ever again. They had taken to trekking during half the night and sleeping the rest of the night until sunrise. During daylight hours they made sure to travel stealthily, keeping within groves of trees and crawling in between shrubs and long grasses. Their caution, it seemed, was not warranted as they were yet to see a single soul in their travels since leaving the outskirts of Caltha's township of Lellban. Since the day they had met, they had journeyed in a north-easterly direction, according to her compass. The potatoes had run out after the first few nights, much to Caltha's chagrin. Rafaella cursed her lack of supplies, wishing for a moment that she had thought to bring some dried beans or corn for the journey. Since the food had run out, they had taken to eating the roots of the wild cattail plants lining the river, cooked like potatoes. Rafaella remembered Wes describing all the wild foods you could find if you knew where to look. Caltha grumbled and complained that the cattail roots weren't as good as real potatoes, and the hairy chickweed leaves that tasted like corn silk made an unpalatable accompaniment, but the food was warm, and sustaining, and it would do for now.

The moon was almost full, providing ample light to move around without the risk of bumping into rocks or bushes. This night they had been particularly lucky in their foraging, discovering vast patches of wild asparagus stretching out across the plains, swaying in the gentle breeze. The asparagus looked nothing like the short, succulent ones Wes used to grow in their garden. This new kind were almost as long as the cattails, and they were thin and reedy, like a green version of wheat. Nevertheless, they filled their satchels with their bounty and when they couldn't fit any more, they took to cutting down bunches and laying them in piles, securing each pile around the middle with the twine from Rafaella's satchel.

"This is far too much to carry." Caltha complained, as they trudged back to their fire, nestled in a grove of trees to provide cover from predators, both animal and human. The fire had reduced to a dull glow and Rafaella moved to layer some more sticks on top of the coals.

"You'll thank me when you're hungry a month from now. Wild asparagus is really good for you, Wes told me. We should eat lots of it tonight, then load up with a few more bunches tomorrow."

Caltha grumbled some more, laying the asparagus on a flat stone and cutting each bunch into small, bite size pieces. She then loaded as many as she could fit in the simmering pot and waited, fists on either side of her face, pushing her cheeks forward sulkily.

When it was ready, Caltha and Rafaella quickly devoured the lot, making lots of humming noises along the way.

"That was really good!" Caltha smiled, patting her scrawny stomach. "I could eat that stuff every night."

"That's good because I think we're going to. Unless we can find some other things to eat."

"Not more cattail roots!" Caltha whined.

"I like them. They fill you up, just like potatoes."

"Yes, well you just don't know what tastes good and what doesn't."

"I do so."

"Do not!"

Rafaella sighed. She was supposed to be the responsible one and here she was, having a silly argument with a six year old.

"Look. We'll try and find some more food tomorrow. Something that isn't cattail roots. Okay?"

Caltha looked at her skeptically, uncrossing her arms and slumping to the ground in a cross-legged position.

"Yeah. Okay. I suppose so. Ooh. I want something sweet!" Her eyes grew bright in the moonlight. "My Ma used to cook strawberries and serve them with cream. It was only sometimes, but I remember them because they tasted so good. She used to grow them out the back in her garden, a traveller once came through with seeds and she made sure to get some. I think she traded a sweater she knitted. He seemed pretty happy with it, he said it would keep him warm on his travels."

"I want something sweet too. I really miss desserts." Rafaella thought of Wes, and his stewed rhubarb. She missed Wes' cooking, but most of all, she missed the stories he would tell as they sat by the fire after dinner.

"Do you think we can find something? Maybe some berries?"

"I don't know. Wes told me you've got to be careful with berries, some of them are poisonous."

"How will we know? I don't want to get poisoned!" Caltha sat upright, alarmed at the prospect.

"It's hard to describe. I know some of the poisonous ones, like pokeweed. The berries are shiny and they look almost black. Some plants just look poisonous, I guess you can just tell."

"But how can we be sure?"

"I'm not exactly sure. I think there's one with five leaves as well. I don't know what it's called. But you can look at some berries and they just don't look like you should eat them. Wes used to tell me only eat the berries you know, like blackberries, blueberries and strawberries, don't try any of the new ones. So I guess we just don't try the new ones. That makes it easier I guess."

"I guess so." Caltha made a face. "I like strawberries the best anyway!"

"Yeah, I can tell that." Rafaella smirked.

"You wait. If we find some strawberries, well, we can't do them with cream, but they are good just on their own. Oh, I hope we find some!"

"Okay, that sounds good. Let's get some sleep first, then we'll go looking in the morning."

Caltha shimmied under the blankets and thunked her head down, taking up most of the satchel with her head.

"Hey, move over!" Rafaella nudged her in the ribs.

"You move over!" Caltha poked back at Rafaella's shoulder.

"Oh, why are you so..." Rafaella took a deep breath, calming herself. "Okay, you have one half and I have the other half. So neither of us takes up more room. Okay?"

"Okay, fine, okay," she grumbled, shifting ever so slightly to the side. Rafaella edged her head over to the side of the satchel and fought her annoyance at Caltha by mentally running through the things she was happy about today. They had found some wild asparagus, the blankets were warm, the fire was toasty and they might find some berries tomorrow. She nudged her shoulder slightly to move Caltha off her side of the satchel. Caltha huffed but finally relented, edging back the tiny distance to her own side.

Wild asparagus, warm blankets, toasty fire. Berries.

39

Another week went by, they had almost completely run through the asparagus and Caltha was clearly having trouble keeping up with Rafaella's brisk pace. The evening was mild but Rafaella could feel the cold weather on the horizon. The air was crisper and the chill clung to the rocks and the damp ground. Maybe a month from now they would be forced to find a more permanent means of shelter than a fire and blankets on the ground. Thankfully, there had been little rain, and their nights had remained mostly clear and dry.

This night, the moon was dim, so it made walking a little more difficult than usual. The light reflected off the slowly moving water, providing some much needed illumination to find their way along the river's edge.

"Ow!"

A loud wailing started up, jarring Rafaella from her thoughts.

Rafaella turned to see a small dark lump in the place where Caltha had been walking. She shuffled back through the blue tinged darkness to find Caltha lying huddled in the grass, knees to her chest.

"What happened?"

"I banged my foot on a rock and twisted it. It hurts!"

"Damn it Caltha! We've still got a few hours of walking time left!"

"I can't!" she said between sobs, her wails growing increasingly louder. "It hurts!"

"Okay, okay. Shh, you have to be quiet, we don't want anybody to hear. Come on." Rafaella gathered up Caltha's shivering body and carried her into the adjacent conifer forest by the river.

"You're really heavy. How can you be this small and be so heavy at the same time?" Rafaella put on a smile, masking the cold prickle at the base of her spine.

The trees in the grove were tall enough that they could provide adequate cover in daylight, should they need to stay that long. Caltha whimpered into her shoulder, soaking the fabric and making it sticky on her skin. Rafaella gently laid Caltha down on the ground, rummaging in her satchel for a blanket. She quickly gathered some large twigs and kindling and set about making a fire.

"It really hurts," Caltha said, sniffling from beneath her tangle of blankets.

"Yeah, I know. I'll take a look at it once I've built the fire. I can't see anything otherwise."

Once the fire was alight, she bent down to remove Caltha's boots. The ankle was fiercely red and swollen to twice its normal size, bulbous and shiny in patches. A dark red strip ran from the side of her heel, almost all the way to her toes.

"Oh."

"Is it bad?" Caltha leaned up on an elbow, attempting to take a look.

"No, not that bad. I think you need to rest it. I'll make the dinner this time." Rafaella hurriedly covered the ankle in warm blankets, trying to keep the fear out of her voice. She didn't know what to do if someone broke something. Wes had taught her some things about first aid, but this was too big for her to handle on her own.

"Don't touch it or move it. You need to keep it in the same spot and rest up. So that means no pawing at it." She figured if Caltha didn't actually see how bad it was, then she wouldn't panic. That was the theory, anyway.

Caltha snuggled closer in the sheets, tears drying on her face. "You're going to cook? Blah. I don't know if I'm hungry anymore."

"Very funny. I'll work something out. You rest. That's an order."

"Yes sir," Caltha grumbled, tucking her arm under the satchel and staring into the flames.

Rafaella foraged for food in the underbrush, reluctant to stray from the light of the fire. She stopped under a shaded part of the woodlands and whistled out a low breath.

"I don't believe it." Under her feet were patches of what looked like weeds with little suckers running out, connecting each plant. Dotted within the leaves were bright spots of vibrant, heart-shaped strawberries. Rafaella gathered every single one she could find, using her tunic as a pouch. When she returned she carefully hid them away in a cloth in her satchel.

She cooked up some cattail roots with the last of the wild asparagus and some spicebush, which she had nibbled on earlier and found she rather liked. She continued stirring it together until the contents of the pot resembled a kind of stew.

She brought the pot over to Caltha, handing her a spoon. "Here, dinner's ready."

"Mph?" Caltha's eyes widened at the sight of the unfamiliar meal before her. "What is this?"

"Um, I think I'm going to call it spicebush stew."

Caltha propped herself on one elbow and demolished half of the stew, only stopping to blow on her spoon so she didn't burn her mouth. Rafaella finished it off while Caltha grinned at her.

"That was really good! Maybe you can cook after all." Her face fell. "Oh, but what will I do?"

"Don't worry, you're be back on cooking duty when you're up and about again. Oh... I nearly forgot."

"What? What is it?" Caltha craned her neck, unable to see what Rafaella was doing, digging around in her satchel. Her face broke into the biggest smile Rafaella had ever seen when she saw the mound of strawberries tucked inside the cloth.

"Strawberries? Strawberries! Oh wow! Strawberries!" Caltha clapped her hands, attempting to sit upright.

Rafaella grinned back. "So, are you going to eat them or just talk about them all night?"

Caltha ate one after the other, barely stopping for a breath. Rafaella marvelled at her enthusiasm, considering they had just finished eating such a large meal.

"You eat as much as a grown up."

"Mmm. Strawberries!"

"That's all you can say now. I'm going to have to put up with you answering me in strawberry language."

"Wow. Strawberries! Oh, thank you Raf!"

"Huh?"

"I said thank you! For the strawberries!"

"You're welcome. But I meant what... what did you just call me?" Tears prickled the corner of her eyes.

"Oh. I called you Raf. Don't you like it? I think it suits you."

She refused to let the tears fall, swiping them away while pretending to push her hair behind her ears.

"No, I like it. You can call me Raf. It's just that nobody has ever called me that, except Wes."

"Oh. You miss him." It wasn't a question. Rafaella nodded, putting a hand on Caltha's shoulder and giving it a gentle squeeze.

"You know what? Maybe I should call you Cal. If you want." Caltha nodded back, smiling widely.

"Yeah, I'd like that." She snuggled down under the blankets and shivered slightly.

"Go to sleep now. Rest up."

Rafaella climbed under the blanket, tunic still stained from the strawberry juices. She flopped back on the satchel and looked up at the stars, milky and crowded, stretching out above her like a shimmering blanket.

"G'night Raf."

"Night, Cal."

40

Rafaella and Caltha had made slow progress on their journey north-east. From what Wes had told Rafaella about the surrounding townships of Forkstream Territory, the township of Lellban, Caltha's former home, was the last familiar landmark on their journey. Further north-east, following the slightly winding path of the Elan River, they gathered wild chickweed and yet more cattail roots. Caltha's ankle was not as bad as Rafaella had feared, the angry redness fading to a smudged blue and green, and after a wasted day of rest, Caltha was able to walk, supported by a large stick. Rafaella had tried to carry her on the first day, but found she could not cover enough ground to make the task worthwhile.

Many weeks had passed, as Rafaella and Caltha settled into a routine of walking half the night and resting until daybreak. They were yet to encounter any others on their journey, but they did not take their good fortune for granted. They kept to covered groves, moving stealthily behind long grasses and reeds. Caltha complained about her ankle, the food, and lack of sleep while each night Rafaella built a fire and planned and plotted the next stretch of their journey.

This night, they were afforded little cover, and rather than a grove of large trees, they found themselves surrounded by a smattering of small shrubs and long grasses. They hastily cleared the ground to settle in for the night, Rafaella placing rocks in a circle around what would be tonight's fire pit.

Thankfully, tonight's moon was nearing full strength, and Caltha made her way to the river without incident. Her ankle was improving, and it would not do to slip and fall again. She washed the cattail roots and peeled them with her knife, leg outstretched, grumbling as she went. Rafaella gathered grasses and twigs to use as kindling and the largest sticks she could find. Once the fire was underway and the pot began to simmer, Caltha retired to the blankets, stretching out her ankle and rubbing the spot above her heel.

"How is it?"

"It hurts still. It's gone stiff from all the walking I had to do." Caltha narrowed her eyes at Rafaella.

"You're leaning on the stick when you use that ankle, right?"

"Of course!"

"Not the other ankle."

"Um... I don't know."

Rafaella shuffled closer, edging Caltha further down the blanket.

"It's just, if you use the stick when you're walking on your good ankle, it doesn't really help, does it?"

Caltha huffed, rubbing her ankle some more.

"Do something, Raf. It's achy."

Rafaella carefully removed Caltha's shoe and sock, placing them on a rock to keep them safe from the slightly dampened ground. She sat at Caltha's feet, crossing her legs and leaning forward to take a look. The ankle was no longer as gruesome as it had appeared on that first night. The redness had gone, replaced with light blue and green spots and the swelling was much less visible. The ankle looked a little stiff and lumpy, but Rafaella was confident there were no broken bones underneath. She rummaged in her first aid kit, pulling out a small tin of salve, Wes had told her it was made from a mixture of ground up shining willow bark and cow udder cream. It sounded disgusting to Rafaella's mind, but Wes had sworn by its effectiveness in treating pain, and she had planned to use it on Caltha's ankle as soon as the swelling had gone down.

Rafaella scooped out a chunk of salve, digging out a piece around the same size as her thumb. She smoothed the cream on the lumpy bone at the hinge of the ankle.

"It's cold," Caltha muttered.

"Sorry, it'll warm up in a minute, just be patient." Rafaella continued to spread the cream over the areas that had once been swollen, gently kneading and smoothing as she went.

"It tickles!" Caltha wriggled, trying to get away.

"It doesn't hurt as much now?"

"It's achy and a bit itchy, but not as bad."

Rafaella kept spreading the salve and massaging the area until the sticky mess had been absorbed well enough to make Rafaella's fingers catch as she rubbed. A sly smile crossed her face and she sneakily moved her fingers underneath the arch of Caltha's foot, brushing lightly.

"Aaah! You..." Rafaella moved away, wiping her hands on a piece of cloth and setting the items neatly back in the first aid kit.

"You... did that on purpose!" Caltha cried out in between cackles.

Rafaella packed away the kit and moved to tend to the fire.

"I don't know what you're talking about." She hid her smile, eyes trained towards the large sticks piled up next to the fire.

"You sneak! I'll get you back! I'll wait 'till you're asleep and then I'll tickle you!"

"I'd like to see you try," Rafaella said, smirking back at her.

"You won't see anything! 'Cause you'll be asleep!" Caltha crowed.

"Oh really? Well you..."

They stopped, heads cocked to the side. A low, whuffling sound had broken the stillness of the night, clearly audible over the rushing of the water.

"What was that?" Caltha whispered. Rafaella was frozen in place, poised for action.

Another whuff, and a low bark rang out, followed by a muted growl.

"It sounds like a dog." Caltha was pale. "It's a dog, isn't it?"

A fierce howl erupted, a resonant note, echoing off the rocks and shrubs surrounding their campsite. Rafaella turned to see a huge black form, furry and dense, powerful muscles rippling under thick, matted fur. Its ears were rounded, its huge heart shaped head yawned open in the bright moonlight, displaying four massive, pointed teeth.

"Move! Get the stick!" Rafaella shouted, roughly pushing Caltha behind her. The bear tracked Caltha's movements, eyeing the weakest of the two with interest. It stood on its hind legs, the massive body looming over them, its black fur rippling, a white irregular blaze on its chest, shaped strangely like a bat. Rafaella edged slowly, moving her hand to the side, plucking her satchel from its place atop a flat rock. The bear stood, motionless, eyes following her movements.

"Hey! Hey! Get out of here!" Caltha's voice startled Rafaella from her thoughts.

Caltha had moved to a spot on a high rock where she stood tall, arms and legs outstretched to make herself as big as possible. She wielded the large walking stick in one hand, waving it menacingly in the bear's direction.

Caltha. What are you doing. What are you doing.

The bear startled for a moment, confused. While the bear's attention was distracted, Rafaella gripped the familiar handle of the Amidal, checked the bullets were loaded and threw the satchel to the side. The bear swung its head around to face Rafaella, its massive neck creasing into gleaming rolls.

Rafaella raised her arm to the sky and shot. Once, twice, three times.

Caltha screamed and crumpled on the rock, arms bent at the elbows to cover her head, stick clattering to the ground.

The bear flinched, eyes squinting closed, then fluttering open with a start. It turned to the left, collapsing on to four legs and lumbering off through the underbrush, its formidable hindquarters loping away into the distance.

Rafaella rushed to Caltha, hand on her shoulder to check that she was unhurt. Caltha looked up at Rafaella, pale and eyes unfocused in shock. Rafaella pulled her into a hug, feeling Caltha's tears soaking her shoulder, bleeding through the fabric of her tunic.

When Caltha had calmed, they retired to the blanket before the fire. Both were unusually cold, shivering together by the heat of the campfire.

"Do... do you think he'll come back?" Rafaella shook her head, arm tightly wound around Caltha's shoulder, stroking her arm in a soothing rhythm.

"No. I think we scared him off. I think it was a he, anyway. Wes always told me that bears don't like to be startled, they don't like noise. And we made a whole lot of noise."

Caltha chuckled softly, shuffling closer to the fire to get warm.

"You were pretty brave today, you know. That took some guts to try something as crazy as what you did." Rafaella scuffed at the top of Caltha's head.

"Yeah?"

"Yeah. You scared me as much as the bear, I think."

"Really? You got scared?"

"Yeah, Cal, I got scared. It was a pretty big bear."

"But you shot the gun though. Scared him off."

"Yeah. I think we make a good team. Look how small we are compared to the size of that bear. And we scared him off."

"Yeah. We showed him!"

"Let's not get cocky, though. We were lucky too."

Caltha made a face at the remains of their overcooked meal.

"It's just mush. Can't believe I ate that."

"Yeah, if the bear came looking for some nice food, he'd be pretty disappointed. Unless he really likes the taste of squishy cattail roots."

Caltha chuckled and pulled the blankets up around her shoulders and shuffled down to rest.

"Raf?"

"Don't worry Cal. I'll stay awake. I've got your stick and my gun. He's not going to come back, but I'll keep watch anyway. Now get some sleep."

Rafaella gripped the stick, propping herself up in a seated position, eyes trained in the bear's last known direction. The gun lay in her satchel, handle pointing out, propped on a rock within easy reach. She listened to the snapping and creaking of the larger sticks as they slowly disintegrated into coals, inhaling deeply the scent of fragrant leaves, willing her heartbeat to return to its normal rhythm.

"Thanks, Raf," Caltha murmured, drifting off into sleep, head pressed against Rafaella's arm.

41

Rafaella and Caltha followed the stream, the rushing water the only familiar feature in the rapidly changing landscape. Caltha's ankle was now strong enough to fully hold her weight, though ever since the bear incident she had kept her walking stick with her for good luck.

The plains had given way to rocky escarpments and caves. They passed waterfalls, surrounded by mosses and miles of greenery. Signs of previous habitation were all around, flattened timber, rusted-out trucks, charred remains of what once must have been houses and halls. It was difficult to determine whether this area had once been a township, or if it had been a rural backwater. When they reached a valley, they saw it, nestled between two large cliff faces angled sharply towards each other.

"Raf! Oh, wow! Raf! Come look!" Caltha ran ahead, arms outstretched.

"Cal, wait!" But Rafaella was too late to stop her. She rushed to catch up, hoping that their arrival had not disturbed any unwelcome wildlife. Or worse.

Caltha stood in the middle of the camp, spinning around with glee. Her feet kicked up the leaves that had gathered in huge drifts against every ramshackle feature left standing.

"How is this still here?" Rafaella mused. The dilapidated cabins were dotted around the overgrown winding path, breaking out from a central point. Rafaella headed for the largest cabin, tucked away to the left of the main path.

The main cabin was made entirely from wood, the beams discolored and slightly rotted in sections, small holes poking through the front walls. The left side of the cabin nestled towards the waterfall was partially covered in a thick green moss. The roof was covered in red ceramic tiles, some cracked in fragments and littered around the sides of the cabin.

Caltha sneaked up behind Rafaella, tickling her ribs.

"Haha! Shelter, Raf, shelter!"

Rafaella tussled Caltha into a headlock, ruffling her hair.

"Better than a blanket on wet grass, I guess."

They circled the cabin, observing the windows on either side. They were outward opening, fashioned from wood, rusted hinges most likely stuck in their shut position. Fastened to the right of the front entrance was an intricately carved plank of wood, partially covered by moss and dirt. Rafaella scraped her hand across the sign, digging through the muck to reveal the letters beneath.

"A..ke...che..ta." Caltha sounded out the syllables, trying to fit them together.

"Akecheta," Rafaella said, brushing the dirt from her fingers.

"What does it mean?"

"I have no idea."

"Then how did you know how to say it then?" Caltha challenged.

"I don't know. I guess I'm just good at reading words."

"I want to know what it means!" Caltha groaned, covering her eyes in frustration. "I hate not knowing what stuff means!"

Rafaella put a hand on Caltha's shoulder, bending down to match her height.

"I hate not knowing too. You know what we can do? We can make it mean whatever we want."

"Like what? I don't get it."

"Well, this place is called Akecheta. And since nobody is here, they're our cabins now."

"Yeah...so?"

"So, Akecheta meant something to whoever stayed here before. But now we're here, and it's ours, it can mean something else to us."

"Do you mean like... A..ke..che..ta, that word, however you say it, can mean us? Like Cal and Raf's place?"

"Raf and Cal's place," Rafaella said, shaking her head.

"Ugh. Sometimes I think I'm the big one..." Caltha muttered. "Okay, Ak.e..cheta is our place. Us!"

"Yeah, us!" Rafaella put her arm around Caltha, giving her a playful squeeze. Caltha wriggled out of her grip, giving her a shove towards the door.

"Come on, Raf!"

"Okay, you ready?" Rafaella looked over at Caltha, who was bouncing on her toes, trying desperately to keep still. Rafaella opened the front door, forcing the hinges inward as they groaned in protest.

"Yaaay! Oh..." Caltha's forward charge stopped abruptly in what had possibly at one time been the living room. The wood on the inside was caked with dust, but it seemed in much better condition than the outside, a light pine, lacquered heavily for protection. The floor was filthy. Dust covered the floor in layers, leaves and twigs scattered throughout. Aside from the promising tone of the wood panels, the inside of the cabin was gloomy, curtains hung in mottled shreds, barely held together in one piece. The roof was snaked with cobwebs, with some nasty looking inhabitants lurking in the corners. The only budding possibilities Rafaella could see was a large fireplace, caked with soot, dust and yet more cobwebs, and an old, cast iron stove with four round iron plates and a hinge opening to an oven.

"Well, it's..."

"Yeah, Cal. I know." She pulled out a broom from the corner of the living room, caked with cobwebs and dust. She sneezed violently, handing the broom to Caltha, who promptly set off a chain of sneezing between them from which neither could seem to stop.

They rushed outside, dusting themselves off and sneezing in all directions.

Rafaella repeatedly hit the broom on a short post near the front door, sending more clouds of dust bursting through the air.

"Stop it!" Caltha spluttered, waving her arms. "Can't breathe!"

"Sorry. Just a few more." She continued to bat the broom across the post, until the clouds dwindled to a few specks. Rafaella crouched, coughing, wiping her nose on her sleeve.

"Gimme that," Caltha said, huffing. Grabbing the broom and turning on her heel, she stomped back into the cabin.

42

201's transfer from Epsilon to Omega Circuit was swift. Her new Omega chambers, however, were identical to her former Epsilon chambers. Nonetheless, she was faintly relieved to be away from the fighting ring for now.

She bathed herself in regulation order. She soaped each section, each segment of her body scrubbed until her body felt stripped, raw. She lathered the regulation facial cleanser and cleansed in order, from the top of her face to the bottom, then working her way up again. Fumbling with the shampoo dispenser, she twisted one way, then the other until a large stream missed her hands and flew down the drain. She muttered to herself, attempting to scoop the last remnants from the bottom of the shower. She would not be supplied a refill until the month was ending. She decided against the second application of shampoo, then applied conditioner, waiting the regulation minutes for the moisture to sink in. She soaped again, pushing the image of Morton's sweaty face out of her consciousness.

He's not here. He can't get to me here. I'm in Omega now, he's back in Epsilon. He's not here. He can't get to me here.

She repeated the phrase over and over until she could almost believe it.

"Line check!"

The call came just as she was fastening her deep blue jumpsuit, the only visible reminder that she was an Omega now, no longer an Epsilon Internee.

No longer a Fighter.

Her door sucked open, letting in a gust of sterile air. Her hair tickled her shoulders, barely dry.

"Internees of Omega. We shall now send our gratitude to Pinnacle Officer Wilcox and FERTS, for our daily provision and protection from those who would seek to strike against our Vassals, our Fighters and our Internees."

"We send our gratitude to Pinnacle Officer Wilcox and FERTS."

201 mouthed the words once more, a practised smile fixed in place.

"The following Internees are to present to the testing rooms: 210, 219, 291, 276. All other Internees report to ration room."

201 followed the line to the Omega ration room, stark and white, much like all the other rooms. The large polished metal tables ran nearly the full length of the room, each Internee seated tightly side by side. For a moment she caught herself looking down the line of Internees for 232 before she remembered. The ration Officers placed each tray at each end of the table, each Internee dutifully passing the trays along until they met in the middle. 201 passed tray after tray until her own settled before her.

The tray was also fashioned from polished metal. She saw a blurry reflection of her own face below and scowled.

"201 will never qualify as a Vassal looking like that." 201 turned to see 242 smirking at her, full lips pouting, careful not to frown and cause a crease in her flawless, translucent skin. She tossed her auburn hair over her shoulder and shrugged, nodding at 256, a blonde haired, blue eyed specimen. 256 giggled, turning her head to the side.

"I know, 242. I know," She said, tittering to herself. "Oh, look, she's even got a line there. Is that a line?" 242 pursed her plump lips together, a smirk tugging at the corners.

"It's called a bicep. Vassals aren't supposed to have them." A muffled gasp came from across the table as other Omegas began to take notice. "I heard she came from Epsilon, with all those low AR rated muscle-bound Fighters." 242 looked straight at 201, scrutinizing her from the waist up.

"Maybe she should go back there," 276 piped up. A smattering of giggles welled up from another group of Omegas to her left.

201 shifted in her seat, smoothing her uniform. She stared down at the ration in the middle of her tray, a single pure white, square shaped piece of protein that tasted faintly of the flowers that grew outside her window, many floors below. She pushed it around her tray, then sat back on the bench. Her fellow Omegas shrugged and talked amongst

themselves, discussing grooming techniques and seduction tips with frenzied enthusiasm.

"Did you know, that if you use your lips, just on the outside of the ear..."

"That's nothing, I know if you kneel, just before his release, it..."

"Did Officer Pietro choose you? He chose me last week. I was so excited to try out the new..."

"Wait, what?" Five perfectly groomed heads turned towards 201.

"What do you want?" 244 narrowed her eyes slightly, though not enough to cause a crease.

"You said Officer Pietro chose you. What does that mean?"

244 rolled her eyes, fluffing her light blonde locks. "Yes, of course, he chose me. Why, don't you know?" A round of giggles erupted around her. "Of course you don't, what Officer would ever choose you? You don't even do any of the right seduction techniques! And, you're a 24Y." She added, flicking at 201's insignia. "Nearly over limit." 244 made a tsking noise, swishing her hair to the side and absently smoothing it down with a finely manicured hand. She looked up, studying 201, her face softening into a grin.

"Oh, this should be fun." She sat closer to 201, nudging her to the side.

"Pay attention to what I am about to say. When an Officer chooses you, it means that they desire you. It is the greatest compliment a prospective Vassal can receive."

201 looked up at her, confused.

"I don't expect you to understand, it probably won't happen for you now, but for us..." she flicked her hair thoughtfully "...prospective Vassals, it is a chance to use all the techniques we have learned in preparation for our Vendees. When you are chosen and an Officer signals for you to disrobe..."

201 looked down at the ground, scuffing her foot under the table.

"It did happen," She muttered. "Officer Morton. He told me to strip."

"There, you see! There is still hope for the almost over limits. You must be so proud, knowing that an Officer desired you, chose you to be his."

"No."

"No?" 244 looked horrified. She laughed nervously, looking back at her fellow Omegas who had gone quiet, straining to listen without looking too closely.

"No, I do not feel so proud, knowing that repulsive, sweaty beast chose me. It hurt, and now I feel... empty. Not proud."

"But... I don't understand. Didn't you try anything they taught you? You really missed a chance at practising the seduction techniques? Didn't you even try? Not once?" 244 shook her head.

"No. Was I supposed to?"

"Yes, silly. That's why the Officers choose the ones they most desire. You missed an important chance to learn everything that is important to a Vassal. No wonder you have not yet been sold to a Vendee." She pushed 201's shoulder playfully. "And no wonder you are nearly over limit."

A tear slipped from 201's eye, rolling from the corner to her temple as she hung her head.

"Don't be sad. You missed a chance, but there will be others. Don't worry."

201 shook her head at 244's misguided words of comfort, opening her mouth to speak but failing in the attempt. Another smattering of tears fell directly to the floor as 201 rested her head on her hand, hiding her face from curious eyes.

"Come on, the presentation is starting. You might want to pay extra attention this time." 244 nudged her forward as the Omegas made their way to the presentation room. "And wipe these off. You look frightful."

43

The presentation room was decked out in varying shades of blue, the familiar FERTS logo adorning each wall. The metal lettering stood out in stark relief to the plush blue wall covering, the white and red rounded shape abstractly representing the Vassal's birthing organs. Behind the logo were the letters XX, faintly outlined in a lighter metal. 201 sank into the seat next to 244, earning a glare from 244's usual seatmates. 244 patted her arm reassuringly, then nudged her as the lights dimmed and the screen became illuminated.

"Watch. You have to pay attention if you wish to be a Vassal."

The screen came to life, opening on a scene in a beautiful field, much more beautiful than the dark forest surrounding FERTS. The field was filled with small trees and flowers. So many joyful Vassals, birthers, she corrected herself, were sitting in this field, playing with their Sires. All Sires were dressed in the fashion of Resident Citizens, the ill-fitting dark tunics flapping about their tiny bodies.

"The Vassals are fulfilled, complete," the voice-over droned.

One of the Sires tripped and fell, the dutiful birther Vassal hurrying to pick him up with an indulgent smile.

"See the pride in their eyes as they tend to their Sires."

"A Sire is the most important gift you can give to your Vendee. A Sire is a future money lender, a lawyer, a judge. Perhaps a teacher, a doctor, a Sire can be most anything. A Sire is the future of all Resident Citizens to come. The future of a Sire is bright and bountiful."

201 shifted in her chair, scratching at a stray eyelash. 244 nudged her firmly and pointed to the screen.

"This is the future for all birthing Vassals: Alpha Field." A cooing of gasps sounded throughout the room. 201 watched as 244's eyes grew wide with excitement. The film became grainy, displaying a field that seemed to stretch on forever, dotted with beautiful residences, large and pleasing to the eye.

"Alpha Field is the reward for all birthing Vassals who have fulfilled their duty and provided their Vendee, their distinguished Resident Citizen with a Sire legacy."

"As we all know, only a Resident Citizen, a fully grown Sire can own property, but in Alpha Field your property will be as close to your own as is permitted. Your time in Alpha Field will be restful and full of pleasing activities," the voice droned on. "All birthing Vassals will be provided with the best of wondrous experiences, the height of fine living." More excited chattering broke out amongst the Omegas, rising and falling with renewed enthusiasm.

201 squinted her eyes, still blurry from tears. She watched the birthing Vassals, gracefully walking their Sires, stopping to engage in animated conversation. She studied the insignias on their pure white jumpsuits. 259266, one of them read. 25Y. The next read 25Y, the next read 19Y.

"Where are all those over 25Y?" she muttered. "Surely there is one that is 26Y, 27Y or even more."

"Shh," 244 said, snapping back. "This is important. We need to be silent and watch."

The voice droned on, showing bountiful foods, places to play, to engage socially, to partake in recreation. The Sires scurried amongst the legs of the slender birthing Vassals, their swan-like necks bent in adoring reverence.

"Wait, where are the others?"

"Quiet now," 244 whispered.

"I see Sires, Sires everywhere. Where are the others? The little ones like us. The future Internees, future Vassals. Where are they?"

"Really 201, you ask too many questions. Has anyone told you that before?" 244 had stopped listening, shaking her head and turning her attention to the screen.

"And now a message from our Pinnacle Officer Wilcox." A chorus of sighs and gasps arose from the presentation room. A man appeared, surrounded by a backdrop of spinning FERTS logos and rich, magenta drapery. His head and face were clean shaven, 201 could not pinpoint his age, clearly he was much, much older than any Officer 201 had ever seen, but his face was narrow and quite smooth, with pointed features and narrowed green eyes. His mouth was a thin line that he curled up repeatedly into a practised, welcoming smile. His uniform was silver, unlike all the other Officers. His chest was littered with various insignia that did not show his Y number or any other identifying symbols.

"Internees of Omega. Future Vassals. The time has come for you all to prepare for Vassal selection. This is the most important time for all of you, and I trust you will do your best for the Officers, and for me."

"You will be tested and rated for your final, pre-Vassal assessments, though your attractiveness rating should be safe, considering you are in the privileged Omega Circuit." A couple of nervous giggles rang out.

"You will also be tested on your grooming, your seduction techniques, dutiful activities and sexual availability." His face became stern, eyes appearing to engage with each Internee in the presentation room. "I trust you will all study intensively for this test, and give the Officers everything they require." The stern mask dissolved, his eyes twinkling with mischief as he went on.

"Those of your who are deemed successful will be promoted to Vassal, and given the opportunity to be chosen by a Vendee. Some of the Vendees you will meet will be wealthy, powerful Resident Citizens who can provide you with such wonders of living, such comforts, things you cannot even imagine you could ever have. Will you do this for me, Omegas, will you join the ranks of proud Vassals?"

"Yes, Pinnacle Officer Wilcox!" came the enthusiastic reply. 201 mouthed the words along with her fellow Omegas but her voice remained silent.

44

201 could not settle that night. Her mind would not shut down, chattering and making no sense. She had tried various techniques to calm her mind, but none seemed to be working. She had attempted a manicure this night and was vaguely satisfied with the results. Her hair was tied in a loose plait, so as not to tangle, and she had bathed in regulation order before bed.

"Just a simple electronic device really, quite basic. The radius is small, just past the edge of the suspension zone. But look here, when I sound the siren, the Internee has five to six minutes to return within the perimeter or the charge goes through from the implant marker here, right through to the heart."

The words jumbled through her head, making little sense. 201 could almost picture the man who spoke, he was an Officer... His name began with C. Not much more was clear, it was something important, she knew this, but the significance was obscured.

Her beauty pill sat in its usual tray, forgotten from the morning. She took the pill, and laid back down, trying to focus on the droning music filling her ears.

The music suddenly changed in pitch and slowed in tempo. Before long she drifted off, waves of relaxation radiating from her body.

45

201 dreamed of the forest that night, the wild fragrances intoxicating her entire being. She stood in the doorway of a room she did not understand. It was a room, but held none of the cold marble, polished metal or stone in matching tones of regulation white.

The room was warm, filling 201 with a sense she had not felt before. The walls were wood, soft fabrics and comfortable looking seating surrounded a pleasing fire, radiating warmth as it popped and crackled softly. The windows were covered with a heavy fabric, trapping the warmth inside and casting a pleasing glow over the lone figure settled within.

She was beautiful. She sat, staring at the hearth, deep in contemplation. Her eyes were bright, vibrant, with hints of little crinkles at the corners. Her mouth was wide, a dimple on one side deepening as she rested her chin on her interlaced fingers. She wore a dark cloth over her chest and trousers, much like the Officers at FERTS, though hers were fastened with what looked like some kind of leather. Her boots were also leather, strong, flat coverings like the Fighters wore in the Epsilon ring. Her hair was a dark blonde, looping down her back in a messy plait. It looked as if she had not used a comb or brush for days, perhaps even months, her dirty nails were short and ragged and her right arm sported a woven leather band around her bicep, partially covering a looping scar. As the flames danced over her face, greenish brown eyes focused in thought, 201 thought she was the most perfect thing she had ever seen.

Another entered the room, this one was shorter, with black hair and blue eyes. She was slightly plumper than regulation weight, and perhaps a little shorter than most Internees 201 had ever seen. Her face was rounded with no sharp angles. It appeared she wore no make up at all. Her hair was thick, falling in messy curls around her face. She was similarly dressed in leather pants and a blue tunic that brought out her eyes.

"Adira is asleep now."

The blonde one looked up, nodding.

"How are you feeling?" She settled herself by the fire, hands outstretched to feel the warmth.

"Can't get her face out of my head."

The dark haired one moved closer, placing a hand on her shoulder. "You can't keep thinking about it, Raf." She stared into the flames, blue eyes dancing and flickering.

Raf, but her name was longer than that, thought 201.

Rafaella.

The voice inside her head startled her, and 201 could not understand its meaning. There were no numbers, no Beth. Their clothing bore no insignia.

"You say that. But doing it is another thing altogether. How are the others?"

"They're a little shaken, but ok. Some food and some sleep will do them good." She made her way towards another of the rooms.

"Cal?"

"Hm?" She poked her head around the corner.

"Did you make tea?"

Cal smiled and left the room, returning with two steaming mugs.

The dark haired one also had another name...

Caltha.

Caltha. It seemed a warm name, the sound soft and kind to 201's ears.

The two sat in silence for a while and 201 wondered briefly if this was indeed a dream. If so, it was most strange, so unfamiliar, yet comforting at the same time.

Rafaella tended to the fire and they drank in silence, staring into the flames. She looked up at Caltha, face stern.

"We can't be that reckless again. You know this, the others know this. Either way, I take full responsibility for what happened."

"Raf, you mustn't blame yourself. Everyone knows it, if Liam hadn't broken away from the group like that, we never would have been exposed. What was he thinking?"

Rafaella shook her head, waving a hand dismissively.

"He was spooked, it happens, especially with the new warriors." She turned to face Caltha. "They were mercenaries, Cal. I haven't seen a group like that in a long time."

"We got them, that's the main thing," Caltha mused. "What were they doing around here?"

"The usual, looting. Not much to take though, must have been on their way somewhere."

"Liam is so sorry, he's sick with it. He'll never forgive himself for Dina. He's just a kid, Raf! I don't know why he was out with us in the first place."

"He has to learn sooner or later. No good hiding him away from it. It happens. I should have ordered him back sooner."

"Raf, it was a skirmish. This is what we do. That's what you taught me, anyway. You can't be everywhere at once." Cal rested the mug on her knee, picking at a stray thread on her trousers.

"It's not good enough!" Rafaella smacked her hand on her knee. "I should've known this would go bad. I had a feeling, and I ignored it. That was my mistake. They should never have been allowed to get in that close to Dina. She was a good warrior. And a good friend." Rafaella's eyes watered but no tears fell.

"Ma?"

Caltha turned to the doorway to see a tiny figure sleepily rubbing her eyes. Dwarfed by the doorframe, she wore a long fuzzy tunic and warm coverings on her feet.

201 stared, unable to believe what she was seeing.

It's a little one. Not a Sire. She's like me, only tiny. No uniform, no insignia. What is the meaning of this?

"Adira! What do you think you're doing?"

201 tensed, anticipating the blow that never came. Caltha rushed towards Adira, playfully scooping her up in her arms, patting her back. "What is it? Could you not sleep?"

"I had a bad dream." She scratched at her messy, shoulder length hair. It was dark and thick, like Caltha's. Caltha placed a kiss on her cheek, seating her on her lap in front of the fire.

Rafaella turned with a grin. "Hey kiddo."

"Raf!" Adira shuffled off Caltha's lap and ran enthusiastically into Rafaella.

"Oof! That hurt. You're getting strong, Adira." Adira clung to Rafaella, tugging at her arm.

"I used a bone dagger for the first time today!"

Rafaella glanced a look at Caltha, raising an eyebrow.

"How'd you go?"

"Good! Lina said I need lots of practice but I can do it! I want to be a warrior when I get big."

"You'll be a good one. I can tell."

"I want to be like you, Raf," Adira mumbled, looking down at her feet. Caltha's eyes darted to Rafaella's, squinting fondly.

"Come on, Adira. You want a story?"

"Yeah!" Adira climbed up on Caltha's lap once more, snuggling into her side.

"Which one?"

"Um... Hett and Wenda!"

Caltha leaned towards a pile of bound papers. She chose one and Adira closed her eyes, a smile creeping on her lips. Caltha's eyes squinted as she grinned down at her.

"The Adventures of Hett and Wenda." She opened the pages. "Long ago, in the township of Palomore, lived two sisters, Hett and Wenda..."

201 did not understand this exchange at first. It seemed so foreign that she could not accept the scene before her. Nevertheless, 201 listened, entranced by the gentle rise and fall of Caltha's voice, the way her voice grew excited in some parts, and the masterful way her voice changed slightly for each of the different voices of the people in the adventure. Adira opened her eyes from time to time, smiling into the fire with a distant look on her face. 201 could see it all unfolding in her mind, Hett and Wenda fighting off hordes of mercenaries in far off places she could scarcely imagine, fighting for things that 201 did not understand. They spoke of strange notions, 'sisters', and 'family', and 'home'. 201 felt a twinge in her chest when she heard that word.

Home.

It was like something long forgotten, perhaps something that once held meaning to her, if only she could find a way to remember. It felt warm, like sleeping, like that moment where you wake and forget where you are, forget who you are, traces of another time lingering like a phantom cloak.

46

"Line check!"

201 shuffled out, the last to fall into line, tugging at the fastener on her jumpsuit that refused to sit straight. After the FERTS Requital, the Officer read out the daily listings.

"The following to report to the testing rooms. 207, 266, 251, 201. All other Internees proceed to ration room."

201 dragged her feet making her way to the testing room. It was another of the indistinguishable sterile white rooms, filled with yet more burnished metal. Titan was waiting for her inside, resting against a metal bench.

"201," he whispered.

201 froze, shoulders stiffening as her eyes darted around the room. She paused, breathing sharply as she gathered up the will to speak. Her voice failed on the first attempt. She took another breath and began again.

"Titan. I guess I should thank you for recommending my promotion to Omega." Titan was not supposed to be in Omega and Epsilon simultaneously. This meant that he had followed her, and this could only mean one thing. 201's breath wheezed out from deep within her chest. She began to unfasten the clasps on her jumpsuit, tugging the sleeve roughly over her shoulder, face impassive.

"Wait. Stop. What are you doing?"

"I presumed you would want me to strip."

"Why... Why would you think that?"

"Because the last time, Morton..."

Titan's face froze in shock. "No. How could he... Did he hurt you?" His eyes narrowed as he stepped forward.

201 raised her eyes to his, holding his gaze. "Yes. He did, actually. But what does it matter? That's what we are here for. I guess I should be proud that he chose me. It is the greatest compliment," she spat the words out, dripping with sarcasm. "And I suppose I am nearly over limit, so I guess I should be thankful for such a rapid promotion. Was that my price, by the way? To get me into Omega? How wonderful, such a gift. I am so wonderfully, extremely, thankful." She turned her head to the side, eyelashes fluttering, smile turned sharp, her intense gaze never leaving his shocked eyes.

"I didn't know. I mean I knew that maybe... I'd heard stories... I wouldn't have let this happen to you. If I had known..."

"If you had known, it would have made no difference. All the Officers know. I'm surprised you don't. But you are new here."

"I am sorry." Titan's eyes were shining, tears withheld.

"It's what happens here. Just how it works." She shrugged. "So you don't want me?"

"No, not like... I can't..."

201 breathed out slowly, a brief surge of relief welling up inside her. She quickly refastened her jumpsuit, steadying her hands to hide the slight tremors. She sank to the floor and hugged her knees.

"I do not understand you. Why are you so different? You do not behave like the other Officers. You make me feel as if I am also different. Like I am something other than this, something other than a prospective Vassal."

Titan slid to the floor to join her.

"Do you wish to be a Vassal? Don't worry, I won't punish you for speaking out. You must understand that everything we say between us will stay between us. You may not be able to trust anyone else, I cannot speak for the others, but I can speak for myself. And I make that promise to you now. So speak freely." His face was pained, eyes tight, yet his gaze did not leave hers, open and unguarded.

201 looked at him for a time, considering his words. "No. No I do not wish to be a Vassal. I do not want to be a birther, as I feel no connection to birthing concerns. I do not wish to please a Vendee and I do not wish to become a Fighter like 23... Like my former Epsilon fellows. I do not wish to be worker in Kappa and I most certainly do not wish to join the scrapheap at Zeta. So I believe, what I am saying, is that I do not wish to be anything that FERTS might require of me."

Titan was silent, hand rubbing idly over his lips, lost in thought.

"I do not wish to bathe in regulation order. I do not wish to comb, brush and dry my hair, perfuming with fragrant oils, I do not wish to manicure late at night, I do not wish to sit alone in my room, speaking of nothing, to nobody, waiting dutifully for my latest muscle mass and AR rating to come through my printing slot. I do not wish to cover my skin with sticky ointments that stick to my regulation pillow, I do not wish to strip for hairy oafs with sweaty beards who crush me with their weight and hurt me and I do not wish to spend my nights washing and washing, trying to get the stink of him off me..." 201 shuddered as the tears erupted, clutching her belly and curling to the side, tucking her feet under her for warmth. She cried for a time, stomach heaving and stuttering. She flinched as she felt a hand tentatively pat the top of her shoulder. 201 looked up at Titan, face streaming as she steeled her expression carefully to give him a nod. He shuffled closer, wrapping an arm around her shoulders as she held on through another bout of tears. His palm gently smoothed her shoulder, repeating the movement as her tremors began to subside and 201 began to tire and snuffle. She burrowed her head closer to his arm, feeling the churning, shuddering pain dissipate slightly.

When 201 opened her eyes, she did not know how long she had stayed on the floor, wrapped up in that uncomfortable position. Titan had not moved, his hand still smoothing over her shoulder as he noticed the change in her movements.

"You fell asleep." Titan was smiling, she could tell.

"How long?" 201 rubbed at her nose, trying to sniff but finding she could not breathe out of her left nostril. Each breath made a squeaking sound. Titan began to chuckle.

201 glared at him, huffing in a breath that made another squeaking sound. Titan's face broke into laughter and 201 could not stop her own laugh as it burst free from her chest.

"Stop that!" She shoved at his shoulder.

"You're the one squeaking." They descended into giggles, 201's hand smacking the floor as she tried not to look directly at Titan for fear of laughing uncontrollably.

When they finally composed themselves, Titan sighed, leaning his head against the wall.

"I haven't laughed like that in a long time."

201 looked over at him, studying his features.

"I never have."

"Not ever? Not even once?"

"No. I guess I have not had that much to laugh about," she said, her smile turning grim.

47

That night, Pinnacle Officer Wilcox lay awake, the theta sounds reverberating in his mind, flipping his thoughts this way and that.

Blue eyes stared at him from behind his eyelids, blinking intermittently.

Get out of my head, bitch.

The eyes blinked back knowingly.

She had been a scientist at his old facility, he remembered her large, kind blue eyes, still vivid after all these years. She had been his protégée, a brilliant mind to match her beautiful face. Her hair was dark, he used to marvel at the way it fell around her shoulders. Her body was slender, delicate, almost fragile to the touch. And how he ached to touch.

Beth.

Her name was Elizabeth, Beth for short. He loved the way her name sounded on his lips, it seemed to him to simulate the sound of breath, the sound of life.

She had been the one that he would choose to share his dream, the only one who would understand his plan, his methods, his vision of order. For much of their time as colleagues, she had not been receptive to his advances. Over time, he had believed he was winning her over, they had spent time together outside of work, discussing theories and research papers of note. The time had come, Wilcox had decided. He would ask her to be his, she would be the one for him, and they would embark on their life together, united by science, linked by a common goal.

Two nights before he had planned to declare his intentions, he had been deeply absorbed in his work, a basic anatomy study. He had made several incisions, removing the left kidney for observation and laying it on the metal table for further study. He was in the process of removing the pancreas when he heard a gasp in the doorway.

Beth stood rigid, face blanched in the cold, blue lights of the laboratory.

"Wilcox. What are you doing?"

Wilcox turned to face her, hands bloodied black in the cold light.

"What do you mean?"

"This." She gestured, slender arm outstretched, nails glinting. A wheezing breath came from the table, the pallid arm raising up in protest. Beth's eyes widened, mouth hanging open in shock.

"What? She is alive? I suspected... I thought what you were doing was unscheduled, against regulation. But she is alive?" Beth took a small step backwards towards the door.

"But Beth. I thought you understood. I thought I explained all of this to you. This is my work, this is what must be done to find new ways, ways to better our society, ways to improve on what nature has provided. This is the way forward! Don't you understand? Darling, don't you understand what a gift this is?"

Beth took another step backwards, eyes darting to the exit. Her voice was low, uninflected.

"Why did you call me darling?"

Wilcox smiled broadly, waving his scalpel in his bloodied hand.

"Because that is what you are to me, Beth! I was going to wait until Saturday to declare my intentions but the time is upon us, it seems! How random yet how naturally ordered these things are! So I shall wait no longer, my darling Beth. Will you be the one for me? Will you join with me to share our work together, share our lives together?"

Beth stared at him, outrage and uneasiness crossing her features.

"No."

"No?" Wilcox laughed, uneasiness creeping into his tone. "How can you say such things? What do you mean? I will give you everything, what more can you ask for? I have left myself open to you! You must not refuse me!"

"No, I will not join with you. No, I will not share your life. And no, I will most definitely not share your work."

"Beth, darling, once you see, you will understand." He grasped her lab coat, blood smearing outwards from the edges of his tightening grip. He dragged her to the body, still twitching, fingers clasping at nothing.

"See the way the blood moves, the way the heart expands and contracts. This cannot be studied in those who are simply expired. The subject must be functional, to display the full workings of this complex machine."

Beth pulled her hand away, shaking with fury.

"She is not a machine, Wilcox! She is a woman! A human! How can you do this? How can you talk as if she is nothing?" She turned to face him, eyes laced with ferocity.

"You will leave this room now, before I call the faculties to have you removed. I will now attempt to save this woman's life, if there is still time enough. You will not harm another, not while I am here to stop you."

Wilcox pressed the button to lock the door, enjoying the rush of air as it sucked shut. His eyes glinted brightly, a cheerless smile crossing his features.

"My dear Beth, the faculties were abandoned at the beginning of this month. There is no faculty, no authority from which to stop me, so you see, it is pointless. Perhaps you did not know, tucked away, living in your laboratory all this time, the councils, all systems of government have been dismantled. Most of the army has defected, there is chaos in the towns, mercenaries have raided most of the supplies and there are few left, save for our facility. And perhaps, we too have little time left. So I offer again, this union will protect you from the mercenaries. I will protect you. Think, Beth. We will have such a life together, you and I."

Beth stood tall, looking directly into Wilcox's eyes. She smiled, hair falling gracefully over her shoulder.

"Wilcox. I would rather be torn apart by mercenaries than spend one moment more with you. I do not care for you, I do not want you, but most importantly, I do not admire you. I despise your 'work', I despise your methods and I think you are sick. Disgusting, in fact. I can not stand the sight of you!"

Wilcox's smile withered piece by piece, his teeth frozen in place in a snarl, his eyes narrowing, snake-like, as he gripped his scalpel tighter.

"That is unfortunate. Yes, very unfortunate," he muttered to himself, edging forward. Before she could anticipate his next move, he drove the scalpel deep into Beth's heart, hacking downwards until he reached the waistband of her trousers. She stumbled, hitting her back on the cold metal table, clutching her chest to stop the flow of blood.

He caught her in his arms, tilting her face towards him. Her eyes widened in panic, a question buried in their depths.

"Shh. Do not speak." He brought his lips down against hers and gently pulled away.

She stared up at him, shaking, the blood draining from her already pale skin. A smile began at the corners of her mouth as she took a deep, rasping breath and spat into his face.

Wilcox swiped at his cheek, outraged at the insult. When he looked back at her, he was faced with hollow eyes staring through him.

"Beth..." He leaned down to kiss her again but she was already gone.

Wilcox carried her body to the metal table, shoving the previous occupant to the floor. The body protested weakly, hand clutching to his trousers as he delivered a swift kick to her head.

He spread Beth out on the table, carefully removing her lab coat, trousers and undergarments.

She lay naked before him for the first time, pale skin unblemished save for the jagged gash snaking from her heart to her hipbone. If only he had not been so careless. If he had only cut her somewhere unobtrusive, less glaring. But it was of no consequence now.

He leaned down, kissing her the gentle swell of her breasts, caressing her stomach, her thighs, everywhere he had planned to touch, to explore. He lay his head on her chest, breathing in the scent of her, cataloging, memorizing.

"My Beth. Why did you not accept my offer? We could have achieved so much, you and I."

He traced her jawline, finger closing over her mouth as if to subdue any response that may have come from her lips. He rearranged her hair around her face, making it just so. He rummaged through her bag, finding a compact with a mirror and her lipstick. He applied the lipstick, meticulously dabbing it over her lips, careful not to smear or mar his achievement with any bloody drips from his coat.

He rinsed a cloth, listening to the water pattering in the metal sink, smattering his coat and face with backsplashes. He turned to Beth, damp cheeks cooling in the sterile air. He turned to Beth, his Beth, scowling at the offensive streaks crossing her pale flesh. He took the cloth, reverently, and dabbed, soaked and wiped until she was clean once more.

He stood back to admire her form, her grace, the delicate features. All should aspire to be like this. She would be the template, the touchstone. He had so much to do, his fingers ached with the excitement of it, the anticipation of greatness to come. He took one last look at her form, perfect, whole, complete. It was time.

"You must not worry, my darling." He stroked her hair, caressing her neck. "My work will live on. You will become part of my work, my greatest work, perhaps. My darling Beth, I will make you live again."

He straightened, touching her lips and trailing a hand down her chin. He readjusted his scalpel in his grip and began to cut.

48

The next morning, after rations, 201 entered the Vassal evaluation chamber, filled with various Evaluation Officers holding identical clipboards.

"Present, 201."

201 walked in what she hoped was a graceful manner, careful not to slouch, to stand before the Evaluation Rating Panel.

The first Officer gestured to the scanning booth, a large rounded structure with an arched opening, surrounded in the blue lights of Omega. 201 hesitated briefly, then stepped inside, the suction doors closing behind her. She remained motionless, just as Harold had coached her to do during her time in Epsilon. The scanner's blue lights passed over her body, crossing and distorting at every line, every curve.

"201. Remain still for the facial analysis."

The disembodied Officer's voice crackled from outside the chamber. She kept her head steady as the white lights danced over her face, scanning and mapping, calculating angles and configurations. The lights in the evaluation chamber flickered through the resource drain, humming as power restored throughout the complex.

The doors sucked open, allowing 201 to step outside into the cool air. She contained a shiver and stood, facing the panel. The Officers surrounded her, prodding and poking, lifting her arms, turning her to the right and left. They tugged at her hair, checked her teeth, shone lights in her eyes and even checked her fingernails and toenails, flicking and bending each one. Satisfied, the group of Officers stepped back as the first Officer spoke again.

"You will now be assessed on seduction techniques for the final part of the testing procedure." 201 stiffened, attempting to hide her discomfort. He gestured to a small room at the rear of the evaluation chamber.

She knocked tentatively, hoping to hear no response, perhaps a last minute rescheduling, anything but the answer that reverberated from within.

"Come."

201 edged inside, body rigid, forgetting her seduction technique training for the briefest of moments.

The Officer sat at a desk, clipboard in hand. His insignia read Officer Piet, 27Y. His face was surprisingly agreeable for an Officer, clean shaven, a shock of brown hair, pleasing brown eyes and a generous mouth. Nonetheless, his demeanour was slightly arrogant, a flinty edge to his smile despite his relatively young age. He looked at her appraisingly, clearly pleased with her appearance.

It's okay. You can do this. Just get it over with. It's either this or the Epsilon Games Ring.

"Um... hi."

"Yes, 201, right? Come over here please."

201 scrolled through her training, desperately searching for the right technique. She settled on smiling and striding forward to sit on the edge of the desk next to Officer Piet's arm. Officer Piet looked up, amused. He reached a hand out to stroke her arm, tugging at her sleeve impatiently.

201 contained her eye roll and decided immediately that she would not pass the evaluation by putting on a show. She was far too uncoordinated and could not bring herself to project the necessary bravado to engage in such a maneuver. She needed something to cling to, an image, something to make this less unpleasant, less strikingly awkward.

As she looked at her outstretched arm, Officer Piet continuously rubbing his finger along her sleeve, it came to her. The familiar sight of Titan's face appeared in her mind, his kind eyes squinting at her the way they always did when he smiled.

Before she could think of much else, she launched herself at Officer Piet, straddling his lap, running her fingers through his hair, imagining blonde, not brown strands sifting through her hands. Officer Piet made a pleased noise as she kissed him, removing his buttons one by one, dragging her lips over his ear and licking along the rim. Officer Piet sucked in a breath, lifting her to the edge of the desk and tangling himself while removing her jumpsuit and trying to undo his shirt at the same time. The image was amusing to 201 and she kept that thought, the thought that Piet, though not of her choosing, was at least as inexperienced and clumsy as herself. This thought, and the image of Titan's face sustained her through the evaluation as she moaned and gasped in what she hoped was an appropriate manner.

Afterwards, Officer Piet seemed satisfied, grinning at her as he attempted to put his uniform back in the correct order.

"That will be all, 201. Well done."

201 left the room, striding confidently past the row of Evaluation Officers, nodding slightly.

She did not let herself cry until she was safely ensconced in her shower, bathing thoroughly, in regulation order.

49

Pinnacle Officer Wilcox awoke to find a hand clasped around his shoulder. The figure beside him was sleeping, her dark hair obscuring most of her face, her eyes closed, though he knew they would be blue, just like all the others he had chosen. He started, shaking off the hand and pushing the figure to the edge of the bed.

"What are you doing in here?" he demanded.

She awoke, pulling the coverings up to conceal her nakedness.

"You asked me to stay. Said I reminded you of someone. You called me Beth. No one ever calls me that, they only call me 267." She scratched behind her ear, sitting up straighter.

"I never..." Pinnacle Officer Wilcox composed himself. "I always sleep alone. Everyone is well aware of this. You should not be here."

"You begged me to stay. Said I reminded you of 'her'. Who was she? Why was she so important to you?"

"There is no 'her'. I do not deem any one of you 'important', you are all the same to me."

"Oh." 267 looked at him sympathetically. The kindness in her eyes was so intense he could not bear it.

"Officer!" He shouted.

"Yes, Pinnacle Officer Wilcox." An Officer appeared at the door, pose rigid.

"Get out," he said, refusing to look at 267.

"What?"

"I said, get out! I do not wish to see you again."

"But..."

"Out!" he screamed, startling the Officer and 267 alike. 267 ran from the bed, grabbing her clothes as she went.

"Officer, a word."

"Yes, Pinnacle Officer Wilcox."

"267 is now demoted to Zeta Circuit. Effective immediately. Do you understand?"

"Yes, Pinnacle Officer Wilcox."

"Go."

50

201 ran her nightly drills, gripping the door frame between her bedchamber and the bathroom, hoisting herself into the air and back down again, repeating the motion until her mind was clear and still. She ran, crouching to begin, circling the perimeter of her bedchamber until she dropped with exhaustion. She stretched, making sure to include every muscle group, finishing with sit-ups, dropping back to the floor when her body began to fatigue. She shuffled to the bathroom, bathing in regulation order, throwing on a robe and laying flat atop the bedcovers.

201 pinpointed her mind to the hallway surrounding the elevator to Wilcox's quarters. She had taken to practising this exercise before falling asleep as a way to strengthen her mind's abilities, much like her nightly drills and agility training. She couldn't always successfully accomplish the task at will, but some nights were more fruitful, such as tonight. She found that she could track the hallways by projecting her thoughts, mapping out each corner, each turn, each feature. Some nights she could almost imagine she was physically present, seeing, absorbing, experiencing. She pinpointed the guards, two at the entrance to the elevator, two at the exit. She

could feel Wilcox now, his form glowing green in her consciousness. The awareness of his vibration made her uncomfortable, his presence growing stronger, smothering her thoughts and scattering her energies. She pulled away from his form, scanning the halls, once again surprised by the small number of Officers surrounding Wilcox, much as she was astonished at the bare minimum of Officers throughout the complex at FERTS. At line check, in the ration room, the games, the Officers appeared far greater in number, simply by placement and proximity. It made 201 wonder how few or how many were out there, outside FERTS. She scanned the halls once more, carefully noting the routine of the Officers, of Wilcox. She catalogued the now familiar features, the distances and the time between doorways, between stairwells, between floors. Something was coming, she felt it approaching on the horizon. And she felt the urgency, the need to be ready for it, in whatever form it might appear.

51

The days began to blur, beginning with line check, rations, and dreary presentations about the prestige afforded to all those chosen to become a Vassal. She dutifully absorbed the information, conceding to her fellow Omega Internees that the height of accomplishment was indeed achieved by becoming a birther. During the nights, yet more hours were spent studying the seduction manual and the myriad of Vassal grooming regulations.

That night, her studying completed, bathing routine dutifully observed, 201 sat on the cold floor in her chamber, regulation nail file in hand. She dragged the tip along the stone, skin breaking into gooseflesh at the sound. She did not know how long she had persevered, methodically dragging the file along one edge, then the other to sharpen each side evenly.

Exhausted, she slumped back against the wall, pushing the hair out of her eyes. She studied the tip, filed to a deadly point. She grabbed her latest assessment report and dragged the edge of the file along the page, spearing and tearing. It would have to do. She looked at the makeshift weapon in her hands, thought about how easy it would be to just cut along her wrist, let the blood drain out all over the floor. The

Officers couldn't touch her then. She would never have to please a Vendee or an Officer ever again. However something had stilled her hand, poised over her wrist. Her mind clouded, visions swimming to the surface. Feet running, the rhythmic thud of boots on ground. The faces of Rafaella, of Caltha and little Adira, living far from FERTS, free from Officers and Vendees. Titan's face surfaced in her mind once more, his familiar eyes fixed on hers.

Titan.

She felt the now familiar twinge in her chest.

Titan. Why do you never leave my mind?

She knew it was no use. She placed the nail file in its pouch, careful not to cut herself in the process. She stood, knees aching, as she began her nightly drills. She repeated her pledge in her mind as she practised her fight moves, stretched, and ran.

I must be flexible, agile, and swift.

I must be flexible, agile, and swift.

She ran until she ached, lifting her weary body on to the bed, she wrapped herself in the coverings and drifted, lulled by the steady beat of her heart.

52

Her bare feet were silent as she felt herself slinking down the hallway. Dressed only in her robe, 201 felt her way through the halls, impervious to the darkness. She stopped before a door, edges glowing a dull grey, the light seeping out from the cracks of the hinges. A symbol mounted the lintel, an elegantly curved Z, surrounded by the familiar FERTS lettering at the rim. 201 pushed forward, the door swinging open easily, allowing her to pass through unobstructed.

On the other side of the door, was another door. She was facing what appeared to be the same door, a mirror image of how she had stood, just moments ago, on the other side. The door glowed in a brilliant white, light leaking in shards, framing the opening. The symbol on the lintel was much the same as the first, however the Z had become an A. She pushed through the door, stumbling through as the door swung weightlessly open. She found herself once more facing the grey door with the Z logo. She pushed again, only to find herself on the other side, facing the door. She continued to push, swinging the door, spinning, revolving as the letters swam before her eyes.

Z

A

Z

A

Z A Z A Z A

She felt herself spinning, twisting through the sheets without catching on them, hovering above her body, she spun, arms flinging out to stop the momentum, falling through nothing. The bland music piped above her head, muting and rising in volume as she continued to spin. She gathered her energies and pulled with all her strength, narrowing her attention on opening her eyes. After a time, her eyes opened, the spinning tapering into nothing, leaving her in stillness. The piped music filtered through her mind as she willed away the sensation of dizziness and drifted once more into sleep.

53

The next morning she checked her readout from the slot after an excessively scrupulous regulation shower routine. She had paid special attention to every stage of grooming until she was satisfied everything was in impeccable order.

AR – 8.9

Muscle mass – Within regulation limits

Vassal Prospects – Recommend selection

She shook her head, unable to decide whether or not this was good news. She was safe from the Games Circuit for now, and perhaps sale to a Vendee would provide her with protection from the Officers. It was only then she remembered the service duties that would be required from her as a Vassal and her shoulders slumped.

"Line check!"

201 shuffled out with the rest of the Omega Internees. She glanced along the line, noting that most had made an extra effort this day, hair perfectly smoothed, faces immaculately made up. Today was the most important day for an Omega Internee. Today was the day that the Internees came up for Vassal selection.

"Internees of Omega. Prospective Vassals. We will now send our gratitude to Pinnacle Officer Wilcox and FERTS, for our daily provision and protection from those who would seek to strike against our Vassals, our Fighters and our Internees."

"We send our gratitude to Pinnacle Officer Wilcox and FERTS."

"All Vassal prospects to report to the Presentation Hall for selection. All other Internees report to ration room."

The Omega Internees gathered in the Presentation Hall, cooing at the pretty decorations adorning the walls. The walls were white, the floors were white, some exotic flowers dotted the corners of the room along with yet more polished FERTS logos and the coveted Vassal logo. The Vassal logo was a large V, surrounded by FERTS lettering around the rim. 201 stood tall, attempting to hide her lack of enthusiasm. Maybe she had ruined her chances by refusing to follow regulations, perhaps her failure to adhere to seduction techniques would prevent her from ascending to achieve the title of Vassal. But then she remembered, the blood, the fear she had felt, and all she had seen in her dreams. This was the only way forward, and there was no point in giving in at this late stage.

"All prospective Vassals to the Presentation Circuit." 201 walked tall and proud, striding confidently along with the other Omega Internees. Each Internee stepped up to the raised circular walkway in the heart of the hall, parading around in a full circle and exiting alongside the point of entry. 201 contained her fear as she stood behind 242, her auburn hair swishing irritatingly close to 201's face each time she walked a few steps forward. Finally, 242 alighted the walkway of the Presentation Circuit, sashaying confidently around the circle, smiling at the Presentation Officers along the way. 201 waited the nominated thirty beats and stepped up to the walkway, attempting to project confidence and allure as she smiled at all the Officers, careful not to look directly into their eyes for fear of scowling. She flicked her hair to the side, swaying her hips while keeping her back neatly straightened. Her relief rose palpably as she neared the exit steps of the Presentation Circuit, gathering with her fellow Omega Internees for the next stage of selection.

After the last Omega Internee had rounded the Circuit, the Head Presentation Officer stepped up to the platform, gesturing to the gathered Internees for silence.

"The Presentation Circuit selections are complete. The following are chosen as Vassals, effective immediately. 244!"

244 stepped forward, grinning at 201 with a sly wink, tossing her light blonde hair over her shoulder.

"212! 261! 271! 237! 284! 242! 256!" They all turned to look at 201, uniform smirks on their faces, save for 244, who looked a little bemused.

"And 201! All other Omega Internees return to your chambers, you will not be up for selection again until the six monthly repeat Presentation Assessments."

201 breathed out through her smiling teeth and stepped forward with the other Vassals.

A Presentation Officer worked his way down the line of newly promoted Vassals, awarding each with their very own necklace of gold, the Vassal logo hanging proudly from the lowest point in the chain.

Squeals and cries of joy rang out, amongst hearty congratulations.

The Head Presentation Officer stepped forward to speak.

"You have now ascended to the coveted position of Vassal. You have reached the ultimate point in your development. You have made Pinnacle Officer Wilcox and all of FERTS swell with pride. You must now fulfil the duty that you were made to perform. Once you are sold to a Vendee, you will be bestowed with the greatest adulation. Now, go, Vassals, and fulfil your duties."

Now I am a Vassal. It is every Internee's dream to be a Vassal. Why do I feel nothing?

244 leaned over and poked 201 in the ribs. "Congratulations." 201 smiled back, eager to convey her enthusiasm at her selection as Vassal.

All the Vassals were bundled into the atrium area, where they waited for the cart to arrive. As it arrived, the Vassals filed into the cart's cage door, guarded by a Supervising Officer on each side. The Vassals giggled and chatted, excited to be going outside to a real township to meet the Resident Citizens, the prospective Vendees.

"Oh, I hope I get chosen by someone powerful! Can you imagine? What luxury!"

"I hope I get a handsome one."

"Oh, yes! Me too!"

201 leaned her head against the wooden bars of the cage and wondered how easily they might snap with the right amount of force. She ignored the chatter of her fellow Vassals and watched with narrowed eyes, mapping every turn, listening to the hoofbeats of the four horses drawing the cage along the winding road, pebbles flying up from the ground as the cart made slow progress through the rocky plains of the suspension zone.

54

They passed streams and rocky outcrops, dense bushland and vast conifer forests. Occasionally, she caught a glint of long, rusted metal lines running side by side, partially hidden by the undergrowth. 201 spotted what looked like the remnants of dwellings, stripped of resources, leaving only the frames standing. Nestled in between the frames were rusted carts, made from metals and covered over at the top. The wheels were made from some kind of black substance, not the usual wood that 201 would have expected to see. Inside these carts were more wheels, also black. The carts were covered in moss, creepers and dirt, holes poking through where the metal should be. 201 wondered why such transports were abandoned, and the whereabouts of the Resident Citizens who used them. The lands were deserted, not a single Resident Citizen to be found. Some parts of the journey became difficult, as the trail was obscured by fallen branches or small trees. The Township Liaison Officers had to climb down from their perch at the head of the cart to move the obstructions in order to continue. 201 tried to estimate in her head each landmark, attempting to calculate the distance between FERTS and their destination. It was difficult, however, because many of the rocks and surrounding bushland appeared infuriatingly identical.

"201." 244 poked her from across the other side of the cage.

"You've been scowling like that for hours. If you're not careful, you'll stay looking like that and no Vendee will want to choose you."

"I'm thinking," 201 mumbled, losing track of the last distance calculation and chastising herself for such an oversight.

"I know, me too. It's so exciting, I can't wait to be chosen. I just know the most prestigious of the Resident Citizens will take one look at me and select me immediately."

"I'm sure they will," 201 replied absently, studying a smooth rock formation that resembled a face in profile.

244 smiled contentedly, leaning back in her seat, absorbing the compliment.

201 returned to her calculations. Two and a half days so far. Rocky plains, then bushland, then forests, then bushland again, then the rock formation shaped like a face.

The path opened out over the ridge to survey the valley below. 201 could see the faint wisps of smoke from the township rising in the distance. Oaklance. This was Oaklance. It appeared that the township was still a couple of hours away, judging by the mountainous terrain. 201 tapped her fingers on the wooden bench beneath her, pitching between excitement at the prospect of seeing the township for the first time, and the sinking feeling of being chosen by a Vendee and having to perform the duties expected of her as a Vassal. The very idea made her nauseous. She swallowed down the fear rising up within her throat as the cart rolled steadily down the rocky path.

55

Late that afternoon, the cart rolled into the township of Oaklance. There were few inhabitants, a small gathering of Resident Citizens slouched and milled about informally for the arrival of the Vassal cart. 201 calculated the chances of being chosen and found that there were perhaps more Vassals than potential Vendees. 201 studied their faces, trying to ascertain which would be the least unappealing prospect. Looking over at her fellow Vassals she was yet again reminded that she would not be the one doing the choosing.

"Vassals, out!" the Liaison Officer shouted, as the other Officer swung open the door to the cage. The Vassals filed out on to a crude wooden platform and stood, neatly arranged in a straight line, smiling brightly. 201 caught herself frowning again and attempted a large smile, sucking in a breath.

The meagre group of Resident Citizens strode back and forth, poking and prodding the Vassals. 201 had thought there would be more of them, perhaps to defend against the mercenaries so widely reviled throughout the territories.

Is this it? Is this all there is?

A sharp jab in her calf muscle startled her and she scowled at the Resident Citizen below her, forgetting herself. He had an arrogant manner and a fluffy beard that looked incongruous hanging off his young face.

"This one looks a bit too feisty for me," he remarked to his fellow Resident Citizen. "I like them to have a bit of fight but... maybe not that much." The other Resident Citizen chuckled, poking 201 for good measure. He had small, mean eyes and 201 disliked him immediately. 201 glared down at him, narrowing her eyes, boring her gaze into his.

"Yeah, maybe not that one. Too much trouble. Oh, hold on, what's this?" He looked over at 242, leering appreciatively. 242 smiled back, smoothing her auburn hair and looking to the side, showing submission to her potential Vendee.

"Yeah, that one. I'll get the redhead. But I'm going first." The other Resident Citizen shot him a look.

"You always go first. Why do I have to get her afterwards?"

"Because I pay, that's why." He handed over two bags of wool, nodding at the Liaison Officer.

"We at FERTS thank you," the Liaison Officer recited blandly. "Please wait until the sales are completed before taking possession of your Vassal."

A few more Resident Citizens made their Vassal purchases, handing over cider, bags of soybeans, oil and a couple of well crafted swords, courtesy of the township's blacksmith.

A Resident Citizen strode into view as the others parted to allow him access. 201 immediately recognized that he was an important figure in the township of Oaklance.

"Resident Citizen Garron. It is a great privilege to serve you. Do you care for the selection this time?"

Garron fixed his eyes on 201.

"Yes, yes I do."

201 gasped, stumbling back a step. She righted herself before falling over, glaring angrily around. She looked back at Resident Citizen Garron. His hair was black, with flecks of white, and his eyebrows peaked above his eyes in a point on each side. His mouth fashioned itself into a wide, fleshy smirk, wet with spittle. His clothing was immaculate, warm cloth trousers, well-made leather boots and a warm covering tunic, interspersed with leather and what appeared to be gold metal fastenings at the shoulders. 201 could not hide her disgust. She did not want to be sold to this Vendee, this Garron. She momentarily lost concern for her appearance and allowed her true feelings to show through. Her face morphed into a fearful snarl, head bowed, eyes sharp and alert to simulate regulation Fighter pose.

Garron laughed, gently touching the fabric of her jumpsuit as she flinched, pulling her leg away from his wandering hands.

"I like this one." The Liaison Officer moved to push 201 towards her potential Vendee but Garron stopped him with a wave of his hand.

"But not this time. I should like to see her again, perhaps when she has calmed a little."

The Liaison Officer glared at 201 at the prospect of losing a sale to Resident Citizen Garron.

"Wait," Garron called, witnessing the exchange. He looked up at 244.

"I want the blonde one. Here." He gestured in 244's direction. 244 smiled at Garron, turning her body to the side and looking over her shoulder at him, lashes lowered.

"Yes, the blonde one. Lovely. Come." He motioned to the two Resident Citizens behind him as they scurried to fetch his payment for his Vassal. They returned with bags of tobacco leaves and home-brewed whisky. The Liaison Officer seemed pleased with the haul and moved to speak to the gathering.

"Resident Citizens. Those of you who have purchased a Vassal, the Vassal is now yours to do with as you will. Returns can always be made for the reason of dissatisfaction, or if the Vassal reaches the 26Y over limit stage. Should a Vassal displease you and you would prefer not to make a return, as I said before, you have the lawful right, and may do with your Vassal as you wish."

201 stiffened, understanding creeping through her bones. 261 stood next to her, smiling petulantly at not being chosen on this visit. 271, 284 and 237 were pensive, faces tilted towards the ground. They had not been chosen this time. It was the worst kind of insult to a Vassal to be rejected for sale to a Vendee. They stood, deep in thought, running through their seduction techniques, the possible steps that could have gone wrong. 271 nervously fidgeted with her

immaculate auburn hair, wondering why 242, the other redhead, had been chosen and she had been overlooked. 237 pondered why 244 was the blonde who had caught Garron's eye. What could she do next time to make herself more desirable? She had much to do, much to consider. The Liaison Officer continued, addressing the small group with fierce sincerity, eyes bright with pride.

"Resident Citizens. FERTS thanks you for your patronage. Your purchase of your Vassal should bring you much pleasure, enjoyment and servitude. Each Vassal has been specially schooled in seduction techniques to please each of you, the privileged Vendee. An important safety observance. Should your Vassal try to escape from your property, you have been instructed to use the freshly installed Township Restoration Beacon. Please accept the most sincere of apologies from all of us at FERTS for the unfortunate incident in recent months. Pinnacle Officer Wilcox has sent his regards, a payment tribute for the township and the complimentary beacon now placed at your disposal. This will guarantee the speedy recovery of your property. Any further issues will be dealt with on the next visit. Proceed."

The Resident Citizens reached up to claim their Vassals, yanking them down from the wooden platform, some hoisted over shoulders, some stumbling down to ground level, attempting to stay upright as they were unceremoniously ushered away by their new Vendees. 201, 261 and the others returned to the cage, the clasp snicking shut behind them as the first Officer left to procure some cider for the journey back to FERTS. The second Liaison Officer stayed with the cart, guarding the haul from the Vassal sales and the remaining Vassals. When the Officer returned with a large clay jug of cider, the other clacked the leather reins, urging the horses forward for the uphill climb.

56

201 could not stop the thoughts cascading through her head, this new information was almost too much for her to assimilate.

...unfortunate incident in recent months...sincere apologies...complimentary beacon...escape...escape...escape...

A Vassal had escaped. In the past few months.

201 thought solemnly about the reasons as to why a Vassal would attempt to escape her Resident Citizen Vendee. Sadly, it did not require much thought. Images of Vendee Yuri, belt in hand, ran through her mind for the first time since her dream, making her shiver in the evening mist as the cart climbed further towards the summit of the mountain.

271 leaned closer to 201, lurching as the cart skipped on a rock.

"Hey. It's not that bad, you know. Not all Vassals get chosen the first time around. I've already been chosen once before, so I guess it's not so bad for me. Although you being 24Y, it doesn't make it any easier."

201 decided to play along.

"You're not helping." She nudged 271 playfully. "I just got scared, that's all. That Resident Citizen Garron is a little... intimidating."

"I know, 201. He's so powerful, so influential. I would have been flustered as well. Although, I think I would have hidden it much better than you managed. Your face just shows everything! You need to work on that, and your seduction techniques as well," she said, snickering, nudging 201 in the ribs.

"Maybe you could help me? I guess I do need to learn how to keep my real feelings where they belong. Inside, where no others can see them."

"I'll see what I can do. We'll practice in the ration room, I suppose you can sit with me next time, I'll show you some tricks."

"Thank you. That's very kind of you."

"Anyway, you don't need that much help from me. Resident Citizen Garron did pick you after all." 201's face crumpled, tears threatening to spill.

"Oh, 201. There you go again. You've got to hold that sort of thing behind your presentation face. I'll show you later. But there's no need to worry, you are sure to see Garron next time. Isn't that exciting?"

201 felt her face straining to withhold the tears. She straightened, pushing her wretchedness deep down within, willing herself to widen her mouth, squint her eyes in happiness, as if 271's words had caused her some kind of solace. 271 brightened, seemingly convinced. 201 smiled, a genuine burst of warmth trickling through her being. This time,

however, it was not Garron's face that filled her thoughts.

57

That night, Rafaella and Caltha stood before her, though they never acknowledged her presence. 201 had to step back a number of times to avoid being part of a collision between herself, Caltha and a new one, one she had not seen before. Limping through the door, arm draped over Caltha's shoulder, she slumped on a chair, large blanket draped around her shoulders.

"How is she?"

Caltha bent down before her, blotting her leg with a damp cloth. She was pale, sweating and confused. She was covered in dried blood, so much so that it was hard to determine what her clothes had looked like when they were clean.

"Cal. How is she?" Rafaella spoke evenly, hiding her frustration.

"Sorry. I can't tell."

"Mph?" The new one was very thin, with high cheekbones and thick, glossy black hair. The gold chain around her neck clinked and tinkled as she moved.

"What's your name?" Rafaella knelt on her other side, hand on her shoulder.

"She's lost a lot of blood." Caltha shook her head, wetting the cloth in a bowl and returning to the trickles of blood running down her jumpsuit, an untouched patch of white showing in the crease under her knee.

Rafaella squeezed her arm gently, urging the newcomer to look up, eyes unfocused.

"Hey." Rafaella smiled, though the tension bled through her features. "Hey. What's your name?"

"Ugh." She slumped again, head lolling back over the head of the chair, eyes rolling to focus on Rafaella's face.

"She needs water. Cal, grab some more cloth. I'll take care of the leg." Caltha rushed to bring strips of cloth, piled over her arm. In her other hand she carried a small jug of water. Rafaella worked quickly, cutting the clothing around the wound and ripping it away, earning a whine of protest for her efforts. She soaked the first few pieces of cloth in the liquid from the bowl, dripping the bronze tinged concoction on the stone floor. She secured them around the wound on her leg, pulling tightly.

"Ow!"

"Sorry, sorry," Rafaella muttered.

"Cal, do we have any fastenings?" A small pin appeared in her hand. She threaded the pin through the material, covering the sharp tip with a sticky round ball. She then produced three more pieces of cloth, dried ones this time, wrapping them in much the same manner as the others.

"We need more wax." Caltha rummaged in a small wooden box, producing another sticky round ball to hand to Rafaella.

"Beth..."

"Check her for other wounds."

"I did that already," Caltha said, snapping back at Rafaella. "She's got a small cut on her forehead and another on her left arm. They're not bad though." She rummaged through the box again, laying out each item side by side. "Damn it. We need more supplies."

"Beth..."

"You need to check her again! We can't have her getting sick or worse because we missed something."

"Beth!" the voice between them shouted, a hoarse and reedy sound. Both heads turned to face her in unison.

"Beth 259292. 23Y, Vassal, Beta Circuit."

Rafaella turned to Caltha, gripping her arm and giving it a shake. Satisfied, the Vassal nodded, head lolling to the side once more.

"Raf, they're real," Caltha whispered. "They really exist."

The Vassal squinted up at them. Rafaella moved forward, placing a hand on her forehead.

"You came from FERTS." It wasn't a question. "Can you tell us where it is?" Rafaella urged.

"Raf... Leave her alone for a bit."

"The suspension zone. Rocky plains."

"You mean the forbidden territories?" The Vassal shrugged.

Rafaella leapt to her feet, shaking her head in frustration. "Of course, of course, where else would they hide it? It's so simple." The Vassal attempted to sit up, blinking rapidly to clear her vision.

"Who are you? And why are you dressed like this? Where is your insignia?"

Caltha looked at Rafaella, eyes questioning. Rafaella shook her head, leaving the room only to return with a mug, steam rising gently in curls.

"Here. Drink this. It will make you feel better." The Vassal took the mug, taking a sip.

"What is this?" The Vassal scrunched up her face, eyes widening as she sipped again.

"It's called tea," Caltha said, smiling. "You'll get used to it."

"How did you escape? Through the... what did you call it, the suspension zone?"

"Of course not. The Implant Marker would have expired me within minutes. The Ward Beacon hardly ever fails to expire or return an Internee."

"What kind of..." Rafaella interjected. Caltha placed a hand on her arm, silencing her.

"One of the Officers, he told me about it, during, well, after one of our... 'meetings'. The Implant Marker, it's somewhere in here." She gestured down her neck, hovering in the area around her collarbone. "He talked a lot, very useful for me. I guess talking was all he was good for, really. At least, I preferred it that way." She shook her head at the memory.

"So how..."

"I was sold as a Vassal. To Vendee Yuri. In the township of Evergreen. He... hurt me. Hit me so many times I can't remember. He took me most nights, then hit me with his fists, a belt, whatever he could find. He enjoyed it, hurting me. He laughed when he did it. I used everything I had learned from my training, did everything to please my Vendee. But he wouldn't stop. He had no need to stop, I knew that. This is what we are here for, to do all that our Vendee requires. I awoke one night, there was blood, so much blood. He had cut me, but he had fallen asleep before he could finish. I got up and looked at him that night, I was standing over him. He was asleep in the chair by the bed, knife in one hand, a drink in the other. I think it was cider. The drink was leaking out of the side of the cup, he was barely holding on to the handle. And I looked at the drink leaking out on to the floor, and looked at my leg and the blood looked just like it and I couldn't... I just couldn't..."

"It's okay." Caltha patted her forearm gently.

The Vassal smiled bitterly. "This is hard for me, I find it hard to say out loud."

"Go on." Rafaella urged her on, seating herself on the floor, backlit by the fire.

"I took the knife out of his hand. It wasn't hard, he was in a deep sleep. I pushed it into his chest. Then I pulled it out and I pushed it in again, and again. He opened his eyes, and he looked at me, I knew he was going to call out so I pushed a pillow from the bed over his face and I used the knife again, and again. There was so much blood, I knew he was expired but I

235

just kept going. Then I ran, I made it out through the back and just ran. I didn't know where I was going, just kept going in the same direction. The bleeding was bad, I knew I wouldn't get very far with my leg like this." She took a shaky breath. "There will be a scar. There's no going back now, he made sure I would not return to Beta Circuit. But that night, I came to know that he was going to expire me. Maybe not that night, maybe the next, I don't know, but he would have done it."

"How did you find Jotha?"

The Vassal took another sip of her tea, shaking her head. "I didn't. He found me. I tried to stay away from the road, I drank from the river, tried to wash off the blood. His horse startled me, nearly knocked me into the river. When I saw him I tried to run, but I fell. He told me he could help. I didn't believe him but I was too tired to run. He put me on his horse and took me here, to this place." Her head listed to the side, eyes growing heavy.

"Come, you need to sleep." Caltha lifted her to her feet, helping her through to one of the bedrooms, covering her with warm blankets. When she returned, Rafaella had not moved from her spot on the floor, staring resolutely.

"What's wrong?" Caltha joined her on the floor, warming her hands by the fire.

"She'll lead them here. I'm glad Jotha found her but she'll lead them here, to us."

"How can you say that? Aren't you glad we finally know that FERTS is real? That there are more like her? All the stories we heard, the sightings, but to see it for ourselves..."

"Don't you understand? They'll be looking for her. They'll follow her here, to us. Someone will talk."

"Only Jotha saw her. She said this herself. You worry too much."

"That's what I do. I worry so you don't get hurt, so none of us get hurt. You may not be afraid for yourself, but who will care for Adira? She's already lost a father because of reckless decisions." Caltha flinched.

"I'm sorry. That was... I shouldn't have said it like that. It's just I fear that this has started something. We can now no longer do nothing, knowing that FERTS exists. Knowing there are others like her. We know we must help them, this is what we do."

"Yes. I know. We have to help them." Caltha placed a hand on Rafaella's shoulder, smoothing the crinkles in her ruffled tunic. "We have to do something. We have to talk to the others about this."

Rafaella smiled ruefully, shaking her head and turning back to stare into the fire.

58

201 was startled by her door sucking open after ration check. The Officer was of medium height, with a pointed nose and reddish hair. He sneered at 201, removing his Officer's coat.

"Strip, 201."

"You even learned my name. Well done," 201 muttered.

"I won't ask again. And if you talk back, I will make it hurt, just to teach you a lesson."

201 stood in silence, making no move to undress.

The Officer, Ryan, 49Y, growled, charging forward and pushing 201 to the bed. 201 was silent, refusing to cry out or assist him in the removal of her jumpsuit.

The door sucked open again. Harold stood in the doorway, mouth open in surprise.

201 looked at Harold, pleading with her eyes, unwilling to speak for fear of retribution.

"201. I was not aware you had company. I will return later."

201 pushed at Officer Ryan, struggling against the tightening grip on her arms as Harold moved to step back from the doorway.

"No, no, no, NO!"

Harold turned away from 201, face impassive.

"As I said before, I was not aware you had company. I will come back later."

"No! Harold! I will not forget this! I will not forget what you have done!" she screamed after his retreating form as the door sucked shut behind him, Officer Ryan's smug face looming above her.

He removed her jumpsuit roughly, ripping the material and discarding it with scorn. 201 felt herself splitting from her body, her mind breaking away, splintering in fragments once more. She found herself flying through forests, over mountains, the night air cooling her skin. It was just as well. Officer Ryan was an Officer true to his word. And true to his word, he made it hurt.

59

That night, 201 dreamed of a sea of orange. It pulsed and throbbed, moving both in unison and in chaos. It swelled, shrunk, surged and retreated, the dull orange of Kappa Circuit flooding her mind.

A whistle sounded, breaking the silence.

She watched in wonder as dozens of arms raised in unison, swinging down with a loud clacking sound. The mass of figures each held an axe, blades flashing as they came down in jumbled cooperation. Two Officers stood at the head of the group, monitoring, cataloguing, preparing their reports that would inevitably land on Pinnacle Officer Wilcox's desk for his ultimate approval.

It's the wood. The wood for the burners, for the boilers, to keep us warm, to prepare the rations.

The whistle sounded out, sharp and shrill.

The blades raised once more, swinging as they came down upon the rows of logs. The wood splintered on the next swing, cracks echoing through the stone hall haphazardly, out of time.

The forest provides the wood. The Kappa Internees provide the labor, this is how it is done.

The first Officer blew a whistle, signaling to continue work. The blades swung once more, axeheads glinting in the flickering lights overhead.

The Officers take the wood. They take the wood to burn...

She saw it then. Another room with large locks, the bars hidden from view in the next room. The other room, carefully hidden from all Internee fellows from Beta, Omega, Epsilon and Kappa. The few select Officers chosen for this special task were the only ones who knew the true purpose of their mission. She witnessed them supervising, shouting, disciplining the orange figures as they filed past, oblivious of the purpose of their massive task. The Internees ferried back and forth, a line of orange insects, carrying, loading the wood, stacking one by one, piling it up so high that 201 could barely see where it ended.

The furnace. It feeds the furnace. It feeds the furnace to burn, to burn, to burn...

Jolted back to the room of Kappa, 201 reeled, the sea of orange swirled and swung, raising and swiping, jumpsuits bending and straightening.

The whistle jolted her, discordant. Something was wrong with the whistle, it sounded...

Broken.

This time there was no splintering, no crack of metal on wood.

This time she head the sickening crack of metal on bone, the unmistakable crunch, the sucking sound of metal on flesh, on muscle, on brain.

The Officers looked on, oblivious, checking their clipboards and recording their daily notes. The first Officer sounded the whistle once more, the sound was louder now, it sounded so much less like a whistle and more like...

A siren. A beacon. The siren.

A tingling spread throughout 201's body, she began to convulse in her sleep, grasping at the bedcovers to gain some kind of purchase.

The Kappa Internees made no sound, faces impassive, axes firmly planted in sure grips, they swung and released, swung and released, repetitively, rhythmically, stoically. They pressed on, continuing their work just as before.

When the axeheads raised once more, blood slaked from the blades with a sucking, splattering sound, flinging jagged, angular patterns on the stone walls.

60

The main cabin at Akecheta was filled with activity this night. Rafaella and Caltha stood side by side as Jotha, Liam, Petra, Bonni, Symon, Ginnie, Kap, Vern and Beth 259292 crowded around the crudely drawn map, a W drawn to the side of the facility to represent the Ward Beacon.

They all wore similar timepieces, checked against each other for synchronization and accuracy.

"So, uh... what do I call you?" Rafaella faltered, gesturing towards Beth 259292, who looked back at her as if she were simple.

"292, of course!" She rolled her eyes.

"Yeah, of course. 292. Okay. We've got to find you a name, a real name. I guess that can wait until later. Now, where did you say Wilcox's quarters are in relation to this hallway here?"

"Pinnacle Officer Wilcox's quarters are up here." She pointed a long, slender finger at the map, as Caltha carefully drew an X in position. "There's just one door in or out. It's opposite the elevator."

Caltha continued to mark the features on the map, crucial details recorded in black, sharpened charcoal.

"I know this because I visited his quarters many times, he sent for me quite often." For a brief moment, she smoothed her hair absently, catching herself and dropping her hands to her sides in frustration. Her eyes narrowed angrily as she focused her attention on the map.

"There are always the same two guards here, at the entrance of the elevator, and two more here, when you get to the top. The two at the top look meaner, if that helps at all. There are no guards near the stairs, as nobody cares to use them. I doubt anyone's been up those stairs in quite some time."

"Right," Rafaella mused. "So this fits with what we discussed earlier. We bypass the elevator, it's too exposed to be of any strategic use."

Rafaella spread the edges of the map on the floor, weighting the corners with rocks the size of her fist. She gestured to the stairwell, motioning for Caltha to mark a point approximately three quarters of the way to the top.

"Liam, Jotha, Petra, you will take the stairs. Set the first charge to explode near the doorway at the top at 20:00 exactly. That is the time Wilcox sends for one of the Internees, correct?"

"That is correct. 20:00 every night. He sometimes sends them right back, but from what I know, he always sends for at least one, regardless. They must arrive at 20:00, that is the specified regulation arrival time."

"Okay. There are fewer guards than I had expected."

"It will be games night, most Officers will be in Epsilon," 292 interjected.

"That's good. Still, we can't get complacent. Liam?"

"No charging off from the group. No unexpected moves without clearance. I got it." He hung his head down, staring at the floor. Petra reached out her arm, giving his shoulder a reassuring squeeze.

"Make sure of it, a lot depends on this," Rafaella shot back. Petra glared at Rafaella until Rafaella's steady gaze wore her down.

"The second charge at..."

"20:03," Petra, Jotha and Liam replied at once.

"Good. Now remember, that's just the diversion. At some point, word will get out that Officer Wilcox is under threat, leading the other Officers and Guards to this area here." She gestured in a circle around the X Caltha had drawn.

"You all need to be out of there by then." She looked at Jotha, Liam and Petra pointedly.

"No excuses, no hanging back. You get yourselves cornered in this section and it's over before it's even begun. We need you here." She pointed to another section marked with a Z.

"Zeta Circuit, right?" Rafaella looked over at 292 questioningly.

292 nodded.

"Yes. That is the location. That's what Officer Gyron told me. His fellow Officer, Lenn was scheduled on Zeta duty. Only a few Officers are selected for this. They are not supposed to discuss it, but Gyron had given him too much cider that night, he..."

"You better be right about this," Rafaella warned.

"It's true. That's the location of Zeta Circuit. I... I kept the company of both of these Officers. They spent a lot of time talking about it, amongst other things. Zeta Circuit is the location where they keep the ones that disobey or can't work in Kappa any longer. They did not go into detail about what goes on there. Only that... well, those relegated to Zeta are likely to disappear after a time. As I told you earlier, I truly fear that the Zeta Internees are in danger, that is what I have grown to understand in my time with the Officers. They did not tell me as such, I just... Had a feeling."

"Okay. Okay. Like I said, you'd better be right about this. Otherwise we're going to be risking our hides for nothing. Jotha, Liam, Petra, you meet up with Bonni, Symon, Ginnie, Kap, Vern, me and Cal at the entrance to Zeta Circuit. With the power out, if its anything like the facilities Wes used to tell me about, it will be a feature of any power failure that the surge will freeze the locks in position, be it locked, or unlocked. You said the door to the ration supply unit is usually wedged open. That's our main path, our chance to get inside. We're assuming that the doors to Zeta Circuit will be locked, so setting up the charges and blowing the doors will be the only way in or out of there."

"What about me?" interjected 292.

"What about you?" Rafaella breathed out, frustrated.

"What do I do?"

"You stay here with Lina, look after Adira, make sure she doesn't eat everything from the pantry. So, let's go through the plan again."

"But... I came all this way. I expired my Vendee. I have proven myself worthy. Now I want to fight, I want to help. If it weren't for me, you wouldn't know the location of FERTS, let alone..."

"Listen!" Rafaella shouted, banging her palm on the floor. "Did you forget that you have one of those things inside you? We don't even fully know how it works, how it could be affected. You only managed to get away from Vendee Yuri because the township beacon had not yet been installed. You know this! It could kill you!" 292 crossed her arms defiantly, scowling at Rafaella.

"But... you said, the plan was to take out the Ward Beacon at 19:55. No Ward Beacon, no charge. So therefore I cannot be expired when we make our escape through the suspension zone."

"Yes, and what if... and this is a small if, but nonetheless, what if we can't knock it out completely? Or what if they have a backup beacon on standby? These are the things we need to consider and more importantly, the things you need to consider. I cannot let you do this. It is simply too much of a risk, at least until we can get you somewhere to get it taken out of you for good."

"Fine. FINE!" shouted 292. Clearly furious, she stood her ground, making no move to leave the room, instead she fixed her gaze on the map and its details.

"Okay what else do you need? I've got it all up here." 292 tapped the side of her head. Rafaella locked her eyes on 292, regarding her thoughtfully, respect dancing beneath her flinty gaze.

"It is regretful. I should like to have you with us, no doubt you showed a lot of guts with all you had to do to get here." Caltha looked over at Rafaella curiously. It was rare that Rafaella demonstrated any kind of deference to anyone, let alone a newcomer.

"Yeah, yeah. Let's get on with it." 292 pushed her elbows on to her knees, squishing her cheeks in concentration. For a moment, she reminded Rafaella of Caltha as a little girl, waiting for the potatoes to cook by the fire in that moonlit clearing, some thirty years ago. Rafaella smiled a secret smile, glancing over at Caltha, who returned the look with a fond grin.

"Now, let's go through the plan again. 19:50!" Rafaella called out.

"Arrive at suspension zone. Synchronize timepieces." Came the slightly jumbled reply, voices clamoring to blend together.

"19:55!"

"Raf and Cal knock out the power and Ward Beacon with charges."

"20:00!"

"First charge, stairs near Officer Wilcox's chambers."

"20:03!"

"Second charge, same spot, time to get out of there."

"20:15!"

"Regroup at entrance to Zeta Circuit. Prepare to blow doors."

"20:20!"

"Lead Zeta Circuit out the door."

"20:25!"

"Sneak out. Get through suspension zone."

"20:30!"

"Regroup. Arm up and make sure we're not followed!"

"You better make damn sure we've got this. We've got to all make sure we've got this down. Forwards, backwards, learn it right to the last detail. Memorize all the steps. No screw ups. We can't have any screw ups. This has got to go right."

None of them noticed the presence of their twelfth member. The dim figure of 201 stood, cloaked effectively beside the heavy curtains, her form swimming in vibrations, focusing her energy on the plan, learning, cataloging, memorizing.

61

Sitting on the floor of her bedchamber, 201 relaxed, taking a break from her nightly stretches. She pulled her knees up, wrapping her arms around them, shuffling back to lean her back against the wall. She thought of Raf, of Cal, of Jotha, Liam, Petra, Bonni, Symon, Ginnie, Kap, Vern, of little Adira, but most of all she thought of Beth 259292. Former Vassal, former Internee. 292, who had escaped her Vendee, escaped FERTS and somehow found her way to Raf and Cal.

Implant Marker. Ward Beacon.

Was it possible that she could have one of these, buried somewhere within her? She supposed it was likely that all Internees were marked in this way. The thought of something inside her body made her break out in gooseflesh. She ran her fingers over her collarbone, trying to feel for anything that might indicate a foreign object, a point of entry, any hint of what might lay underneath.

Five to six minutes to return within the perimeter or the charge goes through from the Implant Marker here, right through to the heart.

201 shuddered.

I don't want to be expired.

201 went through the plan once more, committing each detail to memory. The map was already seared into her mind, the hallways, directions, marked points of interest, were all clear, glowing strongly in her consciousness. She was getting better at traversing the halls, pinpointing the paths with her mind. She had managed to splice the map with her awareness of the layout, marking all the points in bright blue, overlaying everything that Caltha had outlined on the map. Merging the two, she scanned the halls. She could feel the presence of the Officers guarding the doors, could feel the whereabouts of Pinnacle Officer Wilcox, much stronger now, as if he were a red, glowing figure, illuminated brightly in her mind.

"Now let's go through the plan again," she whispered to herself, echoing Rafaella's words.

19:50 arrive at suspension zone.

19:55 Raf and Cal take out the beacon.

20:00 first charge, stairs near Pinnacle Officer Wilcox's chambers.

20:03 second charge, same spot, get out of there.

20:15 regroup at Zeta, blow doors.

20:20 lead Zeta Circuit out the door.

20:25 sneak out, get through suspension zone

20:30 regroup and arm up.

201 repeated the plan until she was tired of hearing herself think. She wanted to help. Though they had never met, in a sense, she had come to regard Raf and Cal as her companions. 201 wanted to do something that would assist them in their quest,

something   distracting,   something   dramatic, something... terrible.

19:50 arrive at suspension zone.

19:55 Raf and Cal take out the beacon.

20:00 first charge, stairs near Pinnacle Officer Wilcox's chambers.

20:03 second charge, same spot, get out of there.

20:05... no, wait. There was no 20:05. There was no 20:05!

Something was going to go wrong. She just knew it. Something was going to go wrong.

.

62

201 awoke early that morning. She gingerly lifted herself from the bed, wincing as the ache ripped through her. She stood tall, arms outstretched, releasing the tension locked within her body. She made her way to the door frame, crying out as her bruises throbbed in protest. She gripped the door frame, facing her bedchamber, the memory of Officer Ryan etched in the bedcovers. She hoisted herself into the air, back down again, into the air, staring at the spot of blood halfway down the covers. She lifted herself up, down, muscles burning with the effort, rising and falling as the spot stared back at her.

She dropped to the floor, crouched in Fighter pose, leg outstretched, arms relaxed, ready to strike. She folded herself on the floor, stretching, raising to her toes, lengthening, loosening her muscles, narrowing her mind to the single spot of blood.

She ran side to side, touching the floor at each pass, circling the perimeter of her bedchamber, the stain of blood burning, glowing before her eyes.

She dropped to the floor, dripping with sweat, hair plastered to her temples. Entering the shower she bathed in regulation order, cleaning, cleansing, inch by inch, layer by layer, until her skin squeaked. She smoothed her hair, applied her cosmetics and regarded herself in her evaluation mirror.

The words from her seduction manual rotated through her mind, reminding her of her duty as an Omega Internee, as a Vassal.

'A Vassal must project the ultimate ideal of beauty. She must be dutiful and ready to please her Vendee. She must keep her head down at all times, looking up towards her Vendee with reverence. She must understand the ideals of the Vassal. To be beautiful, dutiful and ready to serve and please at all times.'

201 stared into her evaluation mirror. The face in the mirror stared back, head straight, chin slightly forward, hazel eyes glinting and flaring in the early morning light. A slow smile edged across her features, spreading widely to reveal her smooth, white teeth. As she stared at her reflection, a chill began to prickle in the base of her spine, making its way slowly upward.

The face in the mirror winked back at her as she turned away from her evaluation mirror, the door sucking shut behind her.

63

In the ration room that night, the Vassals chatted excitedly amongst themselves, arguing over who had been sold to the wealthiest, most influential Vendee, and who was likely to be sold at the next visit to the township. 201 ate silently, eyes flicking from one Vassal to the next.

"You do not deserve Vendee Garron," 261 snapped at 201. He is the wealthiest money lender of all the town's Resident Citizens. "He has poor taste, I suppose." She shrugged, returning to her discussion about how she planned to serve her new Vendee, Lendan, once she had contrived a way to make herself irresistible to him on their next visit.

201 scanned the room, stopping as she spotted a familiar face. Titan's eyes widened as he noticed her. He was careful to school his features into an impassive mask as she signaled to him to wait for her after the scheduled ration allotment.

201 turned to find 271 staring back at her, a slow smile dawning on her symmetrical features.

"Ah, I see why 201 is so churlish all the time. She has eyes for Titan," 284 cooed, her light brown hair shimmering as she leaned in close to 271.

"He is quite an Officer, on that I must agree with you." 201 raised an eyebrow skeptically. "Such fine shoulders, and that face!" 284 looked expectantly at 201. "Was he good? When he chose you? Tell me!"

"I wouldn't know," 201 shot back.

"You wouldn't? Oh. He did not choose you." She studied 201 with mock sympathy.

"How unfortunate for you."

"He chose me!" 237 gloated, rolling her eyes in a vague approximation of pleasure, her blonde hair, freshly curled, bounced around her head as if connected by invisible springs. "And he was by far the best of all of them. You have missed out, 201. How very sad."

"You lie," 201 said quietly.

"What was that, 201? I didn't quite hear you," 237 challenged.

"I said, you lie!" 201's voice carried above the chatter, silencing the Vassals around her. She lowered her voice, leaning towards 237. "Titan does not do what the other Officers do. He did not take me when it would have been easy to do so, and he most certainly did not choose you. You can speak of the other Officers in any way you like, but do not speak of Titan in this way again."

"Come, 237." 271 stepped in. "201 is just jealous because he chose you and not her. It cannot be helped."

201 ignored them, eating every piece of her regulation protein tonight. She would need her strength.

As the Vassals filed out for the evening, 201 stood closer to Titan, facing the line of Vassals, pretending to wait.

"Titan."

"201."

She saw him out of the corner of her eye. He raised a hand as if to reach out to her, abruptly stopping as he reconsidered his actions.

"You're hurt."

So he had seen the bruise, dark purple, almost black. She felt at her neck, realizing her hair was no longer covering the mark. She smoothed it down, obscuring it once more.

"It is done. We cannot concern ourselves with such things. Not now."

"How can you say that? Who..."

"Listen. I need to tell you something. It is important. I will do something tonight. I will not tell you what it will be but I need you to be gone from here before it happens. Create a story, say your father needs you, whatever you have to say, but make sure you are far from here tonight."

"Okay, yes, I can do that. Why will you not tell me what you are doing?"

"It is not safe. I need you to do something else, this is a lot to ask."

"Go on."

"I need you to never return here. Go back to Ignatia, transfer to another fellowship, do not come here again. Your safety depends on this. Please do not make the mistake of thinking I am not serious."

Titan sucked in a breath. "I will do this only because I trust you. I believe you when you say it is important."

"Oh, one more thing. Do you have a timepiece? And does it keep good time?"

"Yes. The Officers must synchronize before each line check. It keeps good time."

"I need it."

"Fine. I suppose I won't be needing it here, anyway."

"Thank you. You have been good to me, Titan. I will remember you."

"What will you do? Will I see you again?"

"I hope that the answer to that question is yes, but this is something I cannot answer."

"201?" His voice seemed to waver slightly.

"I... care for you, Titan. You need to know this."

"I care for you too," he whispered as 201 slipped into the line of Vassals, blending into the mass of blue jumpsuits, lined up in regulation order, filing out the door in a seemingly endless stream.

64

19:50

The suspension zone behind them, the group of ten gathered near a grove of trees adjacent to the Ward Beacon's crude metal housing.

"Doesn't look like much, does it?" whispered Symon.

"We all know what it does," Rafaella whispered back. "We either knock that thing out or all the Zeta Internees are going to have a very short trip."

Symon nodded, holding out his wrist to display his timepiece, the covering slightly cracked. The others followed suit, synchronizing their pieces to Jotha's time, kept current from his frequent visits to Evergreen's central timepiece.

"We good?" Everyone nodded at Rafaella.

"No moving until the power and beacon are out. We don't know what else they've got up there. Stay here."

Rafaella and Caltha edged to the side of the Ward Beacon, fastening the charges to the sides, top and base of the unit. Rafaella looked up at Caltha, who nodded and raised an eyebrow, signaling the charges were ready, their years of functioning as one apparent in their synchronized movements. They peeled away from the unit, Rafaella lighting the charge and catching up easily to Caltha's strides. Perching behind a large grove of trees, they waited.

And waited.

And waited.

Rafaella turned to Caltha, eyes blazing.

"The wiring. Did you check the wiring?"

"No, but Jotha said the merchant who sold it to him..."

"Damn it, Caltha! This can't be happening! Get the others!"

Caltha signaled frantically, the others hurriedly gathering next to Rafaella and Caltha, faces sombre.

"It didn't go off. I'm going to have to check the wiring. This changes nothing. We still proceed as planned, stick to your schedules. You're just leaving early."

"But why..." Ginny started.

"Because it will give you time to check your own damn wiring! And next time, Jotha, when a merchant sells you something, you check the workmanship personally, you understand?"

"Yes. I'm sorry..."

"No time for that. Get going, all of you. And check your connections! Twice if you have to. Now go!" She pushed at Jotha's shoulder as he glanced back at her.

"Make sure you stay in one piece," she whispered to Jotha as they moved out, leaving the relative safety of the grove.

Jotha, Liam and Petra sneaked through the tree line, heading towards the ration supply unit entrance as a muffled cheer broke out from the Epsilon Circuit, the games well under way.

Bonni, Symon, Vern, Kap and Ginnie stayed within the shadows, heading towards the far side of FERTS, closing in on the entrance to Zeta Circuit.

65

19:50

201 charged through the halls, following the path in the map from her dream. She could feel him now. Wilcox. His presence settling as a heavy weight that permeated her entire being. They would be close by now, if Titan's timepiece was as accurate as he said it would be. She could almost feel them, bright and vibrant, wild like the creatures of the forest, closing in on the stark, bloodless facility. The steady glow of the lights were a constant reminder_ that nothing was certain at this moment, there was no guarantee that any of them had made it through the suspension zone.

They're going to be late. They're going to be late. This changes the plan.

She slowed as she spotted an Omega Internee fidgeting near the hallway exit.

"Wait!"

Internee 294 started, facing her with wide blue eyes, her brown hair shaking as she tried to steady her nerves. Her insignia read 18Y.

"Hi, uh... 294 is it? You were sent for by Pinnacle Officer Wilcox?"

294 looked down at her feet. "Yes, he sent for me tonight. I am to be there at 20:00. I will be late if I don't hurry."

"It's your first time, isn't it? The first time an Officer has sent for you?"

294 blushed, eyes cast downwards.

"Yes," came the barely audible reply.

"Well, you must be nervous?"

"Uh... No," she muttered, unconvincingly.

"Hey, it's alright, you don't have to worry. Pinnacle Officer Wilcox changed his demands for tonight. He decided he wanted someone... more experienced."

294 tilted her face up to meet 201's eyes, a trace of hope swimming in their depths.

"So... get out of here!" 201 grinned, smacking her on the shoulder. 294 needed no more encouragement, taking off down the hallway as quickly as she could manage.

19:55

201 pressed on, rounding the corner to the partially hidden entrance to the elevators. She could feel them closing in, a brightness of spirit inching into her heart.

Change the plan. You have to change the plan. Change the plan. Think!

She halted, taking a moment to catch her breath and stepped into the elevator atrium, smoothing her hair. The two guard Officers regarded her coolly. The first guard was hardened, neck thick and corded, expression blank. The second was slightly younger, his eyes were softer, his manner polished and rigid, yet marginally less threatening than his counterpart.

"Uh, I was sent for?" She smiled, ruffling her hair and turning her head to glance over her shoulder at the first guard in what she hoped was a seductive manner. The first guard tightened his jaw, staring straight ahead. She snaked her arm around him, whispering promises into his ear as her hand deftly flicked against a tiny switch on his belt. She broke away, gently pressing her hand against the second guard, giggling as she smoothed her hand across his shoulder, her other hand coiling around his waist, stroking his side near his belt. He caught her eye, startled momentarily, then disregarded her attentions, staring straight ahead. 201 stepped away in a flurry, feigning embarrassment.

"Oh, forgive me." She tucked her hands deep in her pockets, rocking on her heels You are on duty of course. I was sent for by Pinnacle Officer Wilcox for the night." She arched her eyebrow at the second guard. "Very exciting for me, of course. Oh well, perhaps later, when you are off duty..." His eyes widened slightly as he gave an indistinct nod.

The first Officer turned the key and pressed the elevator button. The slow clicking of the numbers made its way down to their floor as she continued to engage the second Officer.

"I look forward to our meeting later." She smirked at him as he continued his practised stare, face forward.

The doors opened quietly and 201 stepped inside with a little wave. As the doors slid closed in front of her she backed up to the rear of the elevator, hissing out a breath. She hurriedly pushed the button to Wilcox's floor and pulled the second Officer's radio from her pocket, a faint smile crossing her face.

She steeled herself and pressed the button to speak.

"Hello? Hello? Officers? Oh, please someone answer!"

The radio crackled to life. "Who is this?" the stern voice snapped back.

"Oh, oh this is terrible! Someone has broken in! I saw them, they attacked some of the Officers downstairs, then started up the stairs next to the elevator. One of the Officers, he was... he was too hurt to speak, handed me his radio to call for help. If you hurry, you can get them! I heard them yelling, they were after Pinnacle Officer Wilcox. They have all the stairs blocked. Oh, please you must hurry!"

"Is this a joke?"

"Does it sound like I'm joking?" 201 shrieked, the floors lighting up one by one as the elevator made its smooth ascent. She clenched her fists in frustration. "I'm in the elevator now, I got in before they could see me."

There was a pause, stretching on for far too long.

This isn't working. How did I think this could work?

"You're in the elevator?"

"Yes! Yes, I'm in the elevator."

"Stay there. We'll wait for you to get here."

"They'll be at the top before I get there! This elevator is slow, I don't know if you've noticed!"

"We'll wait," came the unwavering reply.

20:00

201 stomped on her radio, destroying it and tucking the broken pieces in her pockets. She paced, clenching and unclenching her fists as the elevator climbed towards the topmost floor. She knew the guards would be waiting on the other side, knew she was finished.

The doors fell open, revealing two glaring Officers.

"What is the meaning of this? Who are you?"

"They're coming!" 201 shouted, flailing her hands in the air. "The stairs, you have to get to the stairs!"

201 pointed towards the stairwell, the guard Officers following her gesture. Then, horribly, both Officers turned their heads slowly in unison, faces skeptical, turning to glare at her.

201 stood in what she hoped was an unthreatening manner, trying to look small, scared.

A large explosion reverberated through the hall, the stairway door blowing apart, splinters flying in all directions.

201 ducked, hiding her relief as she covered her face.

They did it. They actually did it.

The Officers charged towards the door, 201 momentarily forgotten.

She stepped forward, edging towards Wilcox's door. The door swung open to reveal Wilcox's scowling face.

"What is all that noise? Who are you? Where are my Officers?"

"You sent for me. That doesn't matter now, there are intruders in the stairway."

201 spoke slowly, concealing her fear of the sight of Pinnacle Officer Wilcox before her. "The Officers have gone after them. They said you would be safe in the elevator. The intruders chose the stairs instead."

20:03

Wilcox looked at her quizzically.

"They said you will be safe with them downstairs. Come."

"I should wait for my Officers to accompany me. This is highly irregular." Wilcox hesitated.

Another explosion rang out from the stairwell, the Officers' agonized cries echoing into the hall.

"You mean those Officers?" she shouted, gesturing towards the stairwell door.

"They're coming! Come on, please, we must hurry! There isn't much time!" Emboldened, 201 grasped Wilcox's hand, guiding him to the elevator, rushing him through the doors before they closed.

201 stayed her hand, allowing Wilcox to reach forward to press the button for the lowest floor.

The elevator began its descent, numbers flashing metronomically above their heads.

20:05

Five floors down, a colossal bang resounded through the building. The elevator stuttered, dropping sharply, then rebounding to a halt.

The tension drained from 201's shoulders and she turned her head as she hid her smile.

All the light sucked out of the elevator, a whir started up and the flickering lights of the backup generator kicked in. A low buzz permeated the air and 201 caught sight of Wilcox's eyes, wide and pale in the unearthly glare.

66

Wilcox looked over at the Vassal before him, gathering his composure. He would not let some minor scuffle mar his authority, even for a moment. He breathed quietly, evening out his breaths until his heart began to resume its usual rhythm.

"So, Beth..."

"201."

"201, right." Like it mattered. She was one of many, her face was pleasing, surprisingly so. She seemed a little different from the others, but he could not pinpoint the reason behind this.

"Why were you in my elevator?"

"I was sent here. You sent for me, isn't that right? Or did they send me to the wrong place? I'm happy to leave as soon as this thing starts moving again."

Wilcox stilled, skin prickling. She was too... calm. She had become calmer still after the lights went out inside the elevator, even with the noise and the backup generators starting up. That wasn't possible. Unless...

There is something else. Something about the way her dark hair falls over her shoulders, the composure in those eyes. Those hazel catlike eyes. Those eyes that are not blue.

Wilcox struggled to steady his voice to reply.

"I sent for one with blue eyes. You should not be here."

"Ah. I am sorry to disappoint, Officer. Am I not to your liking?"

Wilcox scowled, avoiding her eyes. He would not allow some Officer's administrative screw-up make him paranoid. Yet something about her unnerved him. He could feel her gaze, unwavering and intense.

"You speak too much."

"I know, all the Officers tell me that. I just can't seem to keep quiet. I don't know what it is." She laughed softly, flicking her hair. It wasn't the regulation seduction technique, and something about the tone of her laugh unnerved him further.

"I notice you don't have a Y number on your insignia. Why is that?" 201 ventured boldly, eyes innocent.

Wilcox turned to look at her, disbelieving. "That is my business."

"Funny, I thought the same thing about mine. But that doesn't stop this number showing up everywhere I go. I'm nearly over limit, they say. Isn't that sad?" She toyed with her hair, huffing out a breath.

Wilcox remained silent. He should like to study this one. She was the very template he had been trying to avoid. This aberration showed no signs of compliance. She was defective and must be sent for further testing. Then facilitate demotion to Zeta, effective immediately.

"You do know who I am? You've seen the presentations, I trust."

"Oh, yes, I've been meaning to ask you about them. That... what did you call it? Alpha Field? Where is it, exactly?"

"We have special grounds reserved for Alpha Field. Only birther Vassals allowed," he said, scoffing at the Vassal before him. "You will be unlikely to see it, I would think."

"I know. You are so right. I will never see it."

Wilcox nodded, checking the elevator's display for any signs of movement.

"Because it doesn't exist, does it? It's just a pretty picture to show the pretty Vassals so they'll do what you want."

Wilcox froze, neck going cold. He barely contained the rage in his words, voice pitched low.

"What did you say."

"And Zeta too. Oh, don't worry, I'm the only one who knows it. Even most of the Officers don't know it. You keep the Zeta Officers separate to stop them talking to the others, isn't that right?" 201 looked at him out of the corner of her eye, a smirk forming. "Yes," she went on, as if he had answered her question. "There is no Zeta Circuit. It's quite clever really, you get the birthers, the over limits, the ones that don't comply with your 'regulations' and you... well you just expire them don't you? Yes, I saw the pit, all the bones, piles of them. That's where you want to send me as well, right?" She looked into his face, searching hard for any signs of regret. "Yes, I thought so."

His body coiled in her peripheral vision. She readied herself as he lunged for her, fists flying wildly. She ducked to the side, gripping his arm and sending him into the wall with a crash. She crouched defensively in Fighter pose, eyes relaxed to take in any signs of movement.

Wilcox picked himself off the floor, using the wall as support. He turned fully to stare at her, mouth open in slack disbelief. He suddenly looked very frail, somehow smaller than before.

"How do you..." But he was cut off from speaking, possibly cut off from speaking ever again. The regulation nail file pierced his jugular as 201 pinned him to the wall, face menacingly close to his. His neck throbbed, the nail file stopping the outflow of blood, for now.

"Because I have *seen* it, Wilcox. When you sleep, when the Internees and Vassals sleep, I am seeing. I move in my sleep, I can see, hear, not everything, but enough. It took me some time to understand what I was seeing, but now I understand. This is all your doing. I know about your plan. I know about your solution to the problem, the way of your order. And I know what I am."

She stood to her full height, muscles rippling under her slender arm, eyes glinting in the dim half-light of the generator.

"I am not a Beth, nor a Vassal. I am a woman." With that she yanked the nail file from his throat, allowing the blood to spill freely, cascading down his silver uniform, rhythmic spurts surging in time with his fluttering heart.

He raised his hands to his throat in an attempt to stave off the flow but found himself pinned to the wall, arms held tightly above his head.

"Tell me, Wilcox, because I really want to know. How does it feel to be forced? Do you like it? Do you think I liked it?" Her voice raised in the quiet of the enclosed space, trembling with acrimony. "Do you think I liked to have Morton above me, squeezing the breath out of me, sweaty beard scratching my face? I don't believe you fully understand."

Wilcox struggled against her solid grip, attempting to scrabble for his neck once more.

"Do you think any of the Vassals liked it? Liked you? You are repulsive. You disgust me. And I need you to know this, it is so important." She smiled an indulgent smile, licking her lips, zoning in on the shell of his ear, dragging her lips around the lobe. Wilcox shuddered, attempting to break free once more. She laughed softly, a breathy sound, causing a ripple of arousal and fear to spike through his body. She leaned in further, whispering gently, her breath caressing his face.

"None of the Vassals, none of the Internees liked it. For every time you forced yourself on them, for every time you hurt them, made them empty, made them hollow and small, just remember this. None of them wanted you. None of them ever wanted you. You had them, had them all, and none of them desired you. You taught them to fool, to deceive, to pretend. And that is precisely what they did when they were forced to be there, with you. So, you see, what you received was what you created. A lie. You have no wisdom, no knowledge. And you have no heart. I may not continue after you are gone, but I know it was worth it, to see you expire, just like all the Beths you sent to Zeta."

The blood had slowed to a slow bubble, drooling over his collar, rhythm slowing as his face drained and became ashen.

"Beth..." he sputtered.

"I hope you find her where you are going. Whoever she is. And I hope when you get there, she rejects you, like you rejected her when you created FERTS."

"Beth..." His voice was quieter now, barely a whisper. He dropped to the ground, clutching at his neck in a futile attempt to stop the last beads of blood dripping from his throbbing neck.

The last thing Wilcox saw was her smile. Towering over him, unyielding, beaming at him in exultation.

67

20:03

Petra gasped as fire rained down, watching the Officers tumble down the stairs towards them.

"Get out of the way!" Jotha yelled, pushing Petra and Liam up on the railing, taking hold and hoisting himself forcefully to clear the stairs below. Sparks flew towards his face as he shielded himself, the smell of burning hair assaulting his senses.

The first Officer plunged down the stairwell, limbs at unnatural angles, uniform smoking.

Liam turned his head, unable to stand the sight of the Officer's eyes, wide open and unseeing.

The second Officer followed, sliding down a few steps before shuddering to a halt below their dangling feet. His face was burned away, white eyes and teeth the only features visible in the blackness.

"Come on. Let's move." Jotha began to descend, tentatively stepping over the charred bodies of the Officers.

"I can't." Liam clung to Petra, his young body shaking uncontrollably.

"Come on, Liam. This is no time to be a baby."

Liam refused to move, turning his head away from the Officers in disgust.

"Leave him alone, Jotha. He's never seen this." Petra edged towards Liam, careful not to step on the contorted bodies.

"Hey, hey. It's alright. I've gotcha, come on." Petra gathered him up in her arms. He was no longer small enough for her to carry, but she lifted him gently, slinging him over her shoulder, grimacing with the effort as she followed Jotha down the darkened stairwell.

68

20:15

201 leaned against the wall of the elevator, catching her breath. The silence was unnerving. Wilcox lay slumped in the farthest corner, skin waxen, eyes staring at nothing. 201 avoided the diffuse stare, darting her eyes to the hatch above her head. She gripped at the sides, launching herself from the ground to flick at the fasteners, legs swinging until the clamps sprang free. She dropped back down to the floor, listening intently for any sounds of movement. She knew they would be coming soon, the other Officers would surely have been notified by now. She launched upwards once more, curling her legs underneath her body as she swung her feet to the lip of the hatch, feeling the solid weight of the metal take her weight. She slithered up and swung horizontally, flipping herself over and flattening herself on the roof of the elevator shaft.

Another explosion, ringing powerfully in the distance gently rattled the elevator shaft, raining droplets of oil down upon her.

Placing the hatch firmly in place, she looked to the shaft above, dark metal glinting wetly with grease. She wiped her cheek, smearing the gunk towards her temple. The main lighting was still out, the only sound reaching her ears was the clunking hum of the backup generators churning.

69

20:25

Officers Yarrow and Bonn made their way through the hall to the door of the elevator. The doors were sealed shut, most likely from the power outages currently ravaging the complex. Yarrow wheeled the elevator jack to the sliver of light between the doors, wedging it firmly inside.

"What is going on tonight? I thought I heard something earlier." Bonn unpacked the jacking mechanism from his bag.

"Beats me. I heard there was a power surge or something. Come on. Grab the other side," Yarrow ordered. Bonn took hold of the jack, hammering the pincers further inside the gap. Yarrow began to pump the jack, annoyed at the crude force required to begin the pincers' slow drag on the force of the doors.

"Did you choose any last night?" Bonn was grinning at him, eyebrow raised.

Yarrow continued to pump the jack, the thin sliver of ghostly light beginning to leak from within.

"Yeah. 22 something, I don't know. She had the best..." He stopped, face slack with shock.

"The best what?" Bonn moved closer, peering between Yarrow's face and the door. "What?" He stepped closer, looking at Yarrow in confusion. "What is it?"

Yarrow pointed through the gap. The dim glow within the elevator flickered off, then on once more to reveal a leg, bent at an uncomfortable angle, a large pool of dark blood dampening the trouser leg of the Officer's uniform. The Officer's silver uniform.

"Sound the alarm!" Yarrow shrieked, finding his voice. Bonn took off down the hallway, almost slipping in his haste. "Sound the alarm!" he shouted to nobody in particular, his voice ringing out into the empty hall.

70

20:15

Regrouped at the entrance to Zeta Circuit, Rafaella scanned the warriors surrounding her. Jotha had a small burn at the side of his cheek, hair singed a little at the temple. Liam was pale, Petra's arm tucked tightly around his shoulders as she comforted him.

"Did you check it?" she asked Symon.

"Twice, like you said."

"Do it."

Vern, Kap and Symon gathered around the door, signaling to each other. After a last minute check, Vern and Kap fell away as Symon lit the charge, taking cover with the others.

"If there's anyone on the other side of that door," he yelled, "Get back now! Go! Get Back!" A smattering of feet sounded through the door.

The blast roared into the silence, forcing them to the ground, clinging tightly to each other.

As the smoke cleared away, the group found themselves faced with a crowd of blinking eyes, lost figures, dressed in grey jumpsuits. Rafaella stepped forward.

"We're here to break you out. You want to make it past the Ward Beacon? I suggest you follow right now. We don't have much time."

Rafaella was nearly knocked over by the throng of Zeta Internees clamoring to get out. She had expected resistance, some kind of discussion. Clearly, the Internees fancied their chances with Rafaella and their group over whatever it was they were likely to encounter within the confines of Zeta Circuit. Rafaella led the group, charging through the shadows, weaving them through the tree line, edging closer and closer to the suspension zone. She could hear the heavy footfalls behind her, scores of Zeta Internees, their fragile bodies rushing frantically to keep pace with their battle-hardened group. Once through the tree line, they were exposed, running at full speed, dodging rocks and skidding on pebbles in the desolate landscape. Rafaella spotted the safe marker, a large rock next to a low gathering of flat shrubs, growing in a haphazard circle.

"Stop!" Rafaella called. Some of the Internees kept running, adrenaline taking over their actions.

"I said stop!" Rafaella ordered. The small group of Internees stuttered to a halt at the tone of her voice.

"Gather around. We need to get you to our transport, it's not far now. Jotha here has a cart to take you out of here. We'll get you as far from the suspension zone as possible. After that, we'll stick to the lesser-used trails, it will take a bit longer, but we're unlikely to be followed that way."

She looked around at the assembled group, grey uniforms dusty, caked with dirt and sweat. The Internees looked pale and unnaturally thin, their cheeks hollowed out, blue shadows under their sunken eyes.

"We're going somewhere safe. We'll get you some food, somewhere to sleep. That's all you need to know right now, we'll figure out the rest later. Come on."

Rafaella glanced over at Caltha, who had caught up with her strides, matching her steady pace. She wound an arm around Caltha's shoulders, patting her arm roughly and giving her a squeeze. Rafaella heard the barely audible sigh as Caltha let out a breath, leaning against her. Behind them, Ginnie attended to Jotha's burn, propping him up on a large rock as she dabbed at his cheek. Jotha waved her away in frustration, lifting himself to a standing position. Petra carefully weaved Liam through the gathered crowd, his face almost as pale and desperate as that of the Zeta Internees. Rafaella halted, shuffling Caltha to the side as she ushered the Internees towards the path.

The Zeta Internees filed past, flanked by Bonni, Kap, Symon and Vern. Their faces appeared gaunt in the light of the half-moon, their grey uniforms hanging untidily from their rawboned figures.

A siren sounded out faintly in the distance, barely reaching their ears. The Internees tensed, turning and grasping at each other. As the siren continued, the

Internees looked over at Rafaella, panic welling in their sunken eyes.

"You're out of the perimeter, you're safe. It can't get you now. C'mon, now, you all better get going." She gestured towards the path once more.

As the Internees passed by Rafaella, each of them raised their heads to nod, or simply locked eyes for a moment, unable to smile for now, sending what small regard they could manage as they followed the path downwards.

Caltha nudged Rafaella in the ribs, grinning at the passing line of Zeta Internees as they filtered down the winding path to the waiting transport that would take them far away from FERTS, far from the plains of the suspension zone, loading one by one into the transport for the long journey back to Akecheta.

71

20:25

201 gripped the sturdy railing of the elevator shaft, hoisting herself until her feet rested surely on the rungs. She grasped and clung, using her legs to maneuver herself into stability as she climbed further upwards until finally reaching the maintenance side exit. She swung her body into the small doorway, unlatching the locks and slipping through to the other side. A warning siren blared, the shrill, unfamiliar sound jarring her upright as she banged her shoulder on the edge of the door as it swung shut behind her. She looked down at the cut, a shallow gash, the pale flesh flooding with a deep red.

A scar. Like it mattered now.

She edged along the darkened hallway, the siren throbbing with irritating frequency.

It can't be. Please let it not be the beacon.

She heard footsteps clattering from further down the hall. Slipping into the first door she could find, she closed it softly behind her. She looked over at the resting figure on the bed, roused from sleep by the siren but not fully awake. As the footsteps grew fainter, she slipped outside the door before the figure could turn to face her.

Stepping in shadows, she darted from doorway to doorway, breathing slowly and deliberately, honing her ears for anything out of the ordinary. Before long, she was poised before the side door of the ration supplies unit, wedged permanently open by the ration Operators for frequent breaks and waste removal. The locks were out of their holdings, as expected, and she drifted through, unnoticed.

72

20:40

The door swung back to its wedged position, cushioned by 201's elbow as she eased it back as quietly as possible.

She stepped forward, her feet digging gently into the ground. It startled her momentarily, the familiar clack of her boots on stone and metal dropping out from beneath her.

She was overwhelmed by scents, wet and woody, fragrant and mossy, with a note of something familiar, yet intangible underneath. The siren continued to blare from within the complex, shaking her from her reverie. She sprinted towards a nearby grove of trees, careful to stay in the shadows and keep her movements controlled. She stopped, reaching the edge of the clearing facing the suspension zone. She stepped tentatively forward, siren blaring rhythmically.

This is it.

She pushed through the grove of trees, finding herself on the plains of the suspension zone, feet crunching on the ground below, moving faster, gathering speed, she pushed on, heart thumping with exhilaration she ran, passing rocks, shrubs, feeling the breeze smack against her face, she ran, with all the strength in her legs she ran, and ran, and ran.

Other books in this series:

The Rogue Thread
Alpha Field

Other books by this author:

Demon Veil
Open Doors

Sign up to the Grace Hudson newsletter:
www.gracehudson.net

Twitter: @gracehudsonau

Facebook: www.facebook.com/gracehudsonauthor

Goodreads: www.goodreads.com/gracehudson

Manufactured by Amazon.ca
Bolton, ON

17710169R00176